CH

ROAD TO ROMANCE

A photography competition lands Penny Maxwell far from her job at the village bakery shop into the bright spotlight of fame. But she hasn't counted on the machinations of Robina Trent, who sees her likeness in the newspaper and realises they are virtual doubles. When Robina begins to make appearances in Penny's name, no one else is in on their secret. But little does Penny realise that loneliness and heartache will follow — for the man she loves, pianist Paul Hambledon, is stunned by the deep change in her . . .

CHRISTINE LAWSON

◆

ROAD TO ROMANCE

Complete and Unabridged

LINFORD
Leicester

First published in Great Britain in 1966

First Linford Edition
published 2019

*A catalogue record for this book is available
from the British Library.*

ISBN 978–1–4448–4194–7

Published by
F. A. Thorpe (Publishing)
Anstey, Leicestershire

Set by Words & Graphics Ltd.
Anstey, Leicestershire
Printed and bound in Great Britain by
T. J. International Ltd., Padstow, Cornwall

This book is printed on acid-free paper

1

Penny Maxwell pulled down the blind and closed the shop door behind her. It was early-closing day in Elmdale. The shelves in the baker's shop where she worked were emptied and cleaned to shining whiteness. The floor had been scrubbed. Penny had had her lunch with old Mrs. Drew, who kept the shop, and had left her dozing in a deck-chair in the garden at the back.

Now, with the whole afternoon before her, Penny swung lithely along the little street, which still had cobbles, trees lining the edge of the wide pavements, and seats under the trees. The sun shone brilliantly and the air was sweet with the scent of blossoms in the plant tubs outside the hairdresser's where her friend, Sylvie West, was employed.

Sylvie was working this afternoon, so

Penny waved to her as she went by. But the little dressmaker next door, Miss Flora Bailey, called to her as she passed, and Penny went over to her.

'Are you passing the new bungalow at the cross-roads?' Miss Bailey asked. 'I wouldn't bother you, my dear, but I promised this alteration for today. No need to stop and knock. Just pop it inside the porch. Mrs. Ogg'll be on the look-out for it.'

Miss Bailey was a dear soul, with the kindliest of blue eyes.

'Of course I'll take it for you,' Penny said. 'I'm just off to — '

'Don't tell me! Let me guess! The only sale I know of today will be at Tyler's Holt — '

Penny chuckled. 'That's it,' she said, 'They've got a wonderful grand piano, but I don't suppose I'll be able to snap it up. The bidding is sure to be too high.'

'Ah, well, much as I know you want one, my dear, I hope the bidding *is* high. Not only for the piano, but for everything. I feel right down sorry for that family. They've had nothing but a pack of trouble for years past, and now, what with one thing and another, and the poor old man dying and everything being swallowed up in death duties, I just don't see what else they can do but sell out. Poor souls, that house has been in their family for generations.'

'There's no-one left now, though, is there?' Penny frowned.

'There's young Paul. He's the last. A fine young fellow, determined to farm the lands, but, bless you, his heart was in music, and there's no denying it. Right mad the old man used to get. 'There's no money in that fancy stuff!' he'd roar. 'Give your mind to the land, boy, and forget music'. Ah, and the lad would have been a good farmer, too, if he'd not been so pressed with trouble and want of money.'

Penny, whose whole world was taken up with her love of music, understood how Paul Hambledon would feel, though she'd never met him. She, too, had no parents, and had to do a job far removed from music, to earn her living.

'What will he do, then?' she murmured, 'for there's no money in music, as the old man said, unless you can be famous.'

'Aye, and where will you put your grand piano, if so be as you get it, my lass? Can't see 'em getting it into old Bess Drew's place, even if they take the window out.'

'Oh, I shouldn't have it there, of course,' Penny said quickly. 'Mrs. Drew's very sweet, giving me the biggest room but one. But even I know there's no room for a grand piano. No, I'd thought of renting a room at the drill hall, and taking piano pupils. Well, the little ones, first lessons and all that. We haven't got such a thing in Elmdale, now old Miss Parsons is giving it up. I thought it would help my lessons. I'm looking to the future and a diploma.'

'You'd better look to the present and catch that bus,' Miss Bailey said suddenly. 'Here am I, keeping you gossiping. Here's the box for Mrs. Ogg. Come back for a cuppa and let me know how you get on at the sale, my dear.'

★   ★   ★

Tyler's Holt lay back from the road behind a belt of fine old trees. Through the gaps in the trees, the sea could be glimpsed. The house was white, with black timbers, a dark rich lichened roof, small-paned windows; a house to be loved and cherished.

Penny felt sad as she looked at the clustered cars and vans, the sightseers and the dealers, the bills stuck on the walls, the air of hustle and bustle in the cobbled yards.

She drifted with the crowds through the old house, until she came to the music-room where, with the spinet, the harp and a collection of stringed instruments, stood the grand piano.

She caught her breath with the

thought that if the bidding was slack, she might stand a chance.

She stood, while the people milled by, and for a brief moment she was alone by the piano. The sun, filtering through the window, played on her thick dark hair, bringing out the sheen in an almost blue light. That was how Paul Hambledon first saw her, her face in shadow, her glorious dark hair framing her small head.

She wore her new cotton dress, white with a fine black stripe. He wore riding breeches and an open-necked shirt, and he leaned casually on the piano, his thin, tanned face creasing up into a companionable smile.

'Penny for them?' he offered.

'That's my name!' she said in surprise, and then laughed as she realised what he meant. 'Oh, I was thinking about the piano. *I want it.*'

'Just like that, eh? I hope you get it. I can only bear to part with it to someone who feels like that about it.'

Then she realised who he was.

'Oh, it was *yours*,' she breathed, flushing a little.

'Don't be too eager,' he warned her. 'Let the bidding ride for a bit,' and then, before they could say any more, the crowd surged back into the room, in the wake of the auctioneer.

Penny had been to a good many sales, in her quest for a piano, and she knew from the first that she didn't stand a chance. There were too many dealers there, and she heard someone say that the man who was pushing it higher was there on behalf of a concert pianist. But for Paul Hambledon's sake, she was glad that the final figure reached was a good one.

'I'm sorry about that,' a voice said in her ear, and she found Paul Hambledon beside her. 'If it means anything at all to you, there's a sale at the Priory in a fortnight's time.'

'It's all right,' she said huskily. 'I'm used to disappointments. But I'll get the piano I want some day.' And before she realised how it came about, she was

7

sitting beside him in the deep-padded window-seat, telling him about her dreams of a life of music.

'Why haven't I met you before?' he asked with a sigh.

Penny smiled sadly. They hadn't really got a touching point, she in a cake-shop, and he up at Tyler's Holt. She was about to say so, and to ask him what he was going to do now, when they were interrupted.

'Paul! I've been looking everywhere for you!'

The girl was tall and very fair. Her hair, ash-blonde and immaculate, was twisted into a loose knot at the nape of her neck, and she wore a grey tailored dress, with a jade handbag and sandals. She flicked an insolent glance over Penny.

Paul had jumped to his feet.

'Audrey, dear, I want you to meet — ' he began, looking enthusiastically at Penny; but the other girl brushed aside his attempt at an introduction.

'Paul, darling,' she said briskly, 'the

auctioneer wants you at once.' She took his arm, turning her back on Penny as she did so. 'Do come along.'

Penny flushed and got up. Paul started to say something to her, but she didn't catch it. The other girl was determinedly talking, so that he shouldn't have a chance to detain Penny, as she fled down the little staircase behind the half-open door nearby.

She had no idea that he had been with the other girl, or she wouldn't have allowed him to stay there talking to her, encouraging him, to tell him about her plans and her life. What a silly she was to think for a moment that he could really be interested. He must have been just whiling away the time, until his girl friend came and found him.

She found a bus just starting up in the lane beyond the house. She sprinted for it and jumped on to the platform, just as it was moving.

Sitting in the bus, watching the fields and the pleasant view of the distant sea slide by, Penny vowed to herself that she wouldn't go to any more sales. It was too heart-breaking to see what she wanted, and not to be able to buy it. No, she'd rent the old upright piano in the drill hall and make do with that. The thing to do was to start building up a list of pupils right away.

2

Miss Bailey questioned her about the sale, as they had a cup of tea together, and she agreed with Penny.

'Well, my dear, I wouldn't be the one to discourage you, but myself, I think you aimed a bit high, thinking of a grand, when any piano would do at first. I don't know so much about music myself but you wouldn't want children to hammer on a fine keyboard, bless them, would you now?'

Penny hadn't thought of that, and it made her feel better. She went to the drill hall the next day, when the baker's shop had closed for lunch. Everyone in Elmdale knew Penny, and it was not only arranged for her to rent the piano and the little room, but her friend, Jim Langley, who worked at a printers', offered to get a few handbills done cheaply for her.

As she came out into the sunshine she decided she would forget all about Tyler's Holt, and the creased laughing face of the young man who had once owned it.

Just as she had made her resolution she saw him, moving away from the list of bus times. Her heart started to race, as he recognised her, and his face creased into that spontaneous smile.

'*Penny!*' he exclaimed. 'I thought I'd lost you! What did you want to run away like that for?'

'But you were with someone,' she protested.

'That was Audrey Bayfield. Her family have been our neighbours for years. She was fed up, as I was, at the result of the sale.' He smiled ruefully. 'I'm studying bus times. I've had to sell my car. I'm a poor man now.'

'Oh, but what will you do without a car?' Penny cried.

'Go to work, like everyone else,' he smiled, dismissing the subject. 'Look, don't slip away again without at least telling me where you live. I don't even know what your other name is.'

Penny started to say that she lived and worked in Mrs. Drew's cake-shop in Elmdale, when she became aware that a long, cream car had drawn up at the kerb and, turning, saw the supercilious face of Audrey Bayfield at the wheel. Penny murmured goodbye and left Paul Hambledon. She didn't think he would have to depend on the bus service, if Audrey Bayfield had anything to do with it!

* * *

Miss Bailey was worried. She had just received one of the very rare letters from her favourite nephew as Penny Maxwell came into the little shop to match some knitting wool.

'Oh, dear, oh, dear, that boy's in trouble again,' Miss Bailey said, with a worried look.

'It's your nephew Mike, isn't it?' she asked, sympathetically.

'That's right. Like a son, he's always been. Just a lovable rascal who's never grown up. It's time I stopped worrying about him, but how can I, when he's always having ideas that get him into trouble?'

'Oh, yes, I remember. He runs a photographic studio in London, doesn't he?' Penny exclaimed.

'He *did*,' Miss Bailey said grimly, 'until that boy got another bright idea — now he hasn't got a studio. Seems he just managed to pay up the back rent he owed, and then got out. Now he's thinking of taking a kiosk at the seaside. Oh, I could shake him, that I could!'

'Oh, I don't know. Those places make good money in the season, don't they?' Penny asked.

'In the season — that's what I *meant*! What does he think he's going to do in the winter?'

Penny matched her wool and thought about it. She loved this little shop, with its double windows, its wool and general drapery, and the little curtained

14

alcove with its long narrow window at the back where Miss Bailey fitted clients she was making clothes for. It was sweet and homely, but it was essentially Elmdale.

'Why don't you have him here?' she asked Miss Bailey.

Miss Bailey was startled. 'Wha — at?' she ejaculated.

'Well, I just wondered if you could let him have one of your windows to put his photographs in, and let him have that big room you've got empty upstairs for a studio.'

'That's my stock-room,' Miss Bailey said firmly.

Penny chuckled.

'Well, we haven't got a photographer's here and it might bring extra business for you.'

She went out of the shop then, leaving Miss Bailey to turn the idea over in her head, until she thought it was her own.

★   ★   ★

Mike, at that moment, wasn't far away. He was on the wind-swept promenade of nearby Sherwood Bay, his straw-coloured hair tousled, and his frank face troubled.

The man with him was from the Town Hall. He looked uncertainly at Mike as they approached a kiosk on the promenade.

'This is the one I meant,' he said, getting out a bunch of keys to open it up.

Mike looked glum, as he waited for the door to be opened.

'When was it used last?' he asked.

'Oh, well, it hasn't been in use recently as you can see,' the man said, with forced heartiness, as the door creaked open and a rush of stale air came out. 'But all it needs is a lick of paint, and your frames to go up with nice pictures on, and — '

' — and a wave of a fairy godmother's wand,' Mike finished, gloomily. 'How much did you say you wanted by way of rent?'

The man repeated his original figure and Mike's gloom increased.

'I'll think about it,' he said, and went over to the railings to stare down at the gulls screaming as they breasted the high tide in search of food.

A gust of wind suddenly tore at a letter he held loosely in his hand, and whipped it away along the promenade. He sprinted after it but a girl who was just propping her bicycle against the kerb quickly took in the situation, and put her foot on the letter as it momentarily scudded along the pavement. She had scooped it up by the time Mike had got there.

'I say, thanks!' he gasped, holding out his hand for it.

She stared down at the envelope.

'Mike Bailey! Oh, but it can't be,' she said, looking at him. 'Yes, it is. I've seen your photograph on your aunt's mantlepiece.'

She gave the envelope back to him, laughing.

'I'm Penny Maxwell. I work in the baker's, next door to your aunt's shop in Elmdale.'

Mike stopped staring at Penny's lovely little face and the rich dark hair that blew across her eyes in the wind, and pulled himself together.

'I say, are you? Well, how do you do?' and they both started laughing. 'It isn't what Aunt Flora would call the best way of getting introduced, but it'll do for me.'

'I expect you've been to see your kiosk your aunt told me about. Was it any good?'

He pulled a face and said:

'No, not really. I'll just have to keep on looking.'

'Well, I have to put a card in a window. I'll have to be getting along,' Penny said, and hesitated. She thought Mike Bailey looked a little lost, but she didn't understand how it was he seldom seemed to go and see his aunt, especially as he meant so much to her. 'We advertise in Sherwood Bay, you know,' she said, slowly. 'People like to come to Elmdale, and it's nice to know a home-made cake-shop where you can get tea in the garden.'

Mike laughed again, unbelieving.

'People *want* to go to Elmdale? What for?'

'It's not as sleepy as it used to be,' Penny told him. 'The parade where your aunt's shop is, does quite a brisk trade. But we haven't got a photographer.' And before he could answer her, she got on her bicycle and rode away to do her errand, having gone as far as she dared in planting the seed of an idea.

★ ★ ★

Mike went over to the rails again. The shimmering blue sea was empty of pleasure boats. The season hadn't started. The pier was being painted, and all the shelters along the promenade were having their roofs silvered to match the pier. Ice cream booths were

19

being painted cream and scarlet, and the picture post-card kiosks were being made ready to open. But at best, it would only be a quiet place, unless someone invested a great deal of money, and made the town popular. Was there a living here for a one-man photographic studio?

He thought of Penny Maxwell, with her bright intelligent face, the warmth of friendship pouring out of her, and it made him feel lonely. He decided to go to Elmdale after all, and see Aunt Flora.

He hadn't seen her for two years. The last time he had seen her he had been in the middle of an idea, and on the verge of making money. He hadn't wanted to stay in Elmdale. Now it was different. He soon found himself enveloped in the kindness and comfort she offered him and, before that day was out, Aunt Flora had persuaded him to take the room over the shop for a studio.

When Penny dropped in that evening

with the things Miss Bailey had asked her to get while she was in Sherwood Bay, she found the little dressmaker full of plans and ideas, and Mike looking less glum than she had seen him on the promenade.

'So, that's all settled,' Miss Bailey declared, 'and I'll be able to see what the scallywag's up to, and whether he's eating the proper food, and if his clothes are aired and his socks darned.'

Mike grinned at Penny. 'See what I mean? I knew it would be like this if I said yes to Aunt Flora's idea. She'll treat me as if I was ten years old.'

'That I won't, my boy! You're going to work for your living. What do *you* say, Penny?'

'Well, I think there's plenty of work for him here,' Penny agreed. 'Sylvie wants her photograph taken. She works in the hairdresser's,' she told Mike, 'and she's very pretty. Most of my young piano pupils would want to be taken, I know.'

Mike screwed up his face.

'I'll take a picture of *you*,' he said, quickly.

'No, not me,' Penny said hastily. 'I don't make a good picture.'

'He's going to take as many pictures as he can,' Miss Bailey said firmly. 'I've thought it all out. We'll get Jim Langley to do some handbills, advertising that for the first week all pictures will be taken half price.'

'Hey, wait a minute,' Mike protested.

His aunt waved him to silence.

'You're in no position to argue, young man. I'm the one who's providing a new camera and materials. I'm not grumbling, but since I shall be a sort of partner in the business, then I have some say. Everyone who orders a portrait in the first week can have it framed for half price.'

'What a wonderful idea,' Penny exclaimed.

'We'll put the first week's best pictures in the window and we'll invite the mayor to have his done free, if he'll let us put it on show — that's always good publicity.'

'Well, let's throw everything in, Aunt Flora, by having a Baby Week. Give everyone at the clinic a chit to get their babies done at cut price.'

'And the best baby picture gets a prize,' Penny chimed in. 'Speaking of prizes for the best pictures, have you seen the competition details from Curly Corn Flakes, the new cereal? They've got a big money prize and a publicity campaign.'

Penny searched in her bag.

'Here's a sheet of details — I got them from the grocer's this morning.' She passed the printed sheet over to Mike. 'You see, the photographer, as well as the model, gets a prize, if the picture wins.'

Mike read it, a new glow coming into his eyes.

'Gosh, I'd like to have a smack at that. Let's see — beautiful girl in a shimmering dress, arranging roses in a bowl.'

'What's that got to do with corn flakes?' his aunt objected. 'A wholesome young woman laying the breakfast, I should say.'

'Take Sylvie,' Penny said warmly. 'She's so pretty, and being blonde she'd photograph beautifully.'

Sylvie was thrilled with the idea.

'What will I wear?' she asked Penny excitedly, as they went through her small wardrobe and discussed the idea.

Penny put her head on one side. Sylvie had blonde, wavy hair and wide, surprised eyes, and a soft, baby mouth. She looked a lot younger than her twenty-two years.

'Something simple,' Penny advised, 'and no ornaments or jewellery. Why don't you leave it to Mike?'

'He's awfully good-looking, isn't he?' Sylvie smiled dreamily.

'Maybe I'd better go and check up on Miss Bailey's shampoo and set appointment for next week,' Sylvie went on, but Penny knew it was to see Mike again, and not Miss Bailey, that Sylvie was so anxious to go down to the photographer's shop.

Mike was pleased to see her.

'I was thinking about how I'd take your picture,' he said. 'A natural background might be effective. Are there any beauty spots around here?'

Sylvie undertook willingly to show him the local countryside.

She looked cool and sweet in the evening light. She was wearing her new dress of dusky pink, dotted with black, and as she leaned over the stile looking down into the water-splash she looked sweetly pensive.

'That's it!' Mike said, enthusiastically. 'Hold it a minute while I consider it.'

Sylvie obligingly stayed like it, and then began to wonder at the silence. She looked round and found Mike regarding her with a curious expression on his face. He flushed as she caught him staring.

'Right, we'll settle on this,' he said, trying to sound businesslike.

The subject of the competition occupied Mike's mind completely, and he went to a great deal of trouble over the lighting on the day he took Sylvie's picture. He had high hopes of the result.

3

When Mike had developed and printed it Miss Bailey looked at it over Mike's shoulder.

'What's that got to do with something you eat for breakfast?' she wanted to know.

'Nothing, Aunt. You just have to give 'em a nice picture of a girl that they can stick on their packets, so people will remember it. That's all.'

'Then take one of Penny. She's pretty enough to remember without water splashes, and all that cluttering up the scene. Here, I'll fix her up for a picture — I can see I'm the one around here with the ideas.'

She hustled Mike out of the studio and sent him for Penny. When Penny came, Miss Bailey was unrolling a bale of cloth.

'What's that for?' Penny asked, mystified.

'Draping cloth is part of my business,' Miss Bailey said briskly. 'I'll show that Mike a thing or two about effects. Now, duck, you just stand up on that platform and leave the rest to me,' and she pinned the cloth so that it hung in rich folds, its pattern catching the light. 'It's a furnishing brocade, and it ought to come out a real treat in a picture.'

Just before she called Mike in, Miss Bailey got out of a little box a long pair of antique ear-rings.

'These were my grandmother's,' she said, fixing them to Penny's ears. 'You won't find another pair like these. Now, I'll just brush all these curls of yours into a bunch high at the back and tie some ribbon through — like a Greek statue, see? Now we'll see what Master Mike has got to say about all that, against a white backcloth.'

Mike said very little when he saw his aunt's handiwork, but he looked thoughtfully at Penny, and got busy with his lighting equipment. Penny was an excellent subject for she had natural poise and wasn't in the least bit selfconscious. When the sitting was over Penny forgot about it.

Sylvie came in to collect her picture when Mike was examining the developed proofs of Penny's. She gasped as she saw the result. It was an unusual picture, bringing out all Penny's warmth and vitality; the classic lines of the hair emphasised the fine modelling of Penny's face, and the beginning of that elusive smile of hers that was haunting as well as gay. The drapery clung to the graceful lines of her slim figure.

Mike was thrilled with the result of his work.

'Is that Penny downstairs?' he said boyishly, as the gay notes of Penny's laughter came up from the shop below. 'Let's get her up here to see what I've made of it.'

Sylvie went immediately, but came back soon after, to say that Penny couldn't stop. She had a piano lesson to give, down at the drill hall.

'And that's all she thinks about her photograph!' Mike said, disgustedly. 'What a girl!'

★　★　★

Penny's thoughts were not on the photograph and the competition, but on Paul Hambledon. He had vanished from the district. Tyler's Holt was to be opened as a training school, but there were hitches. The place stood empty and neglected.

Audrey Bayfield was away, too. Some said she had gone abroad with her mother. Penny had the uneasy feeling that Audrey Bayfield would be where Paul Hambledon was, and he couldn't afford to go abroad.

And so it was with a sense of shock that Penny opened a letter addressed to her one morning, and found that it was from Curly Corn Flakes, about the competition.

She stood staring down at the typewritten letter in her hand for so long that Mrs. Drew asked her if anything was wrong.

'It can't be true!' Penny gasped.

'What can't be true, my dear?' Mrs. Drew asked worriedly, and as Penny still looked blankly at the letter, Mrs. Drew took it away from her and read it herself.

'Oh, dear saint's alive!' Mrs. Drew gasped, and flopped down in the chair behind her. But she quickly recovered. 'My dear, what a splendid thing for you! You've won the competition, don't you see? You and that picture of yours, that young Mike Bailey took! You've won it!'

Penny shook her head in bewilderment.

'But I can't have! I mean, there must have been heaps better than me! What about that one of Sylvie?'

Mrs. Drew's excitement faded a little.

'Deary me, that'll be awkward now, won't it? Seeing as Mike had such hopes of that picture of Sylvie. They do say he's showing signs of getting sweet on her. Oh, well it can't be helped. Here, let's toddle along and see my old friend, Miss Bailey. We've still got a quarter of an hour before we open the shop.'

Miss Bailey already knew about it.

'Mike had a letter this morning, too,' she said. 'I'm very glad for you, Penny. You've deserved it if anyone did. Mike sent in two entries, you see — you and Sylvia — and you've won.'

'But he ought to have told me!' Penny exclaimed, still very bewildered.

Miss Bailey smiled soothingly.

'You just take your good fortune as it comes, lass. What will you do with all that money?'

A smile crept slowly over Penny's lovely little face and a dreamy look came into her dark eyes.

'Now I can have my music,' she said.

Penny knew that secretly Mike would have liked Sylvie to win. He came rushing back from seeing her, and whirled Penny round.

'Penny Maxwell, for heaven's sake, don't you realise? You're going to be someone now! Publicity for you, my girl, good times, the bright lights, the holiday of your life! Look excited, for goodness' sake, or I shall sit down and weep. Here, take a look at *my* letter — we'd better get cracking. There isn't much time.'

'Much time?' Penny repeated blankly.

'Of course. We've got to go to London for the presentation of our prizes, you and me, and we're allowed to take a friend. I thought Sylvie might come as a sort of consolation prize. What do you say?'

'Of course she must come if she can get away,' Penny said warmly.

'Right. Well, we don't have to bother about anything. It's all laid on, it seems. Posh hotel, and they want you to wear the things they've chosen for you, so you can bet you'll be dressed in style, my girl.'

'When can I come back and start on my music?' Penny asked with such a serious expression that Mike burst out laughing.

'What a girl,' he chuckled. 'Let's savour these good things while they last. Then you can think about hard work and all that. Myself, I'm looking forward to some very good connections, all through that photograph of mine. It's going to set me up as a photographer all right.'

He looked fondly over at his aunt, and she nodded.

'I knew I was right, Mike. You can do it if you bring your mind to some real hard work, and I'm not going to let you slack off again, or get into trouble with your mad ideas.'

★ ★ ★

The presentation of the cheques took place in the large concert hall of the Curly Corn Flakes factory. Penny, in the new outfit chosen for her — a slim-skirted white dress and a little white hat with clustered blue flowers in front — stood breathless with excitement on the stage. There were a number of speeches, and she had her photograph taken all over again.

Then they went on a tour of the factory, and Penny was left with the Publicity Agent, Walter Wiley, who was to start right away, building her up into a glamourous young lady who would now be featured on all the Curly Corn Flakes products.

'Now,' Walter Wiley said, with his nice smile, and that manner of his which drew people out to tell him their little confidences, 'just tell me about yourself in your own way. Got any brothers or sisters?'

'I'm an orphan,' Penny confessed. 'I don't even know who my real parents were. Even my adoptive mother is dead.'

'Oh, that's interesting. I can work up quite a story about that. The mystery girl — who are her real folks?'

'Oh, no,' Penny protested laughing with slight nervous deprecation of the idea. 'There's no mystery about me. I was just one of a lot of babies in the Primrose Orphanage in London, and someone happened to want a little girl. That's all.'

'And where have you been living all these years?'

'My adoptive mother came to Elmdale when I was quite little. I'm not sure where we lived before then, but I could find out from Mrs. Drew, if you like. Mrs. Drew keeps the baker's and cake shop in Elmdale. We lived there, until my mother died. Then Mrs. Drew went on looking after me. I worked in her shop.'

'And what are your hobbies?' Walter Wiley asked softly, already racing ahead with his publicity campaign.

'I'm afraid my only hobby is the piano,' and Penny told him a little of her hopes for a musical career.

Walter Wiley sat forward, really interested now.

'That's fine. You shall have that piano. A white one. On a circular platform. You can play — oh, let me think. The gimmick will be The Girl With The Golden Hands. See? Music in her hands — golden — money coming in and — '

'I don't think . . . ' Penny began doubtfully, but he cut her short.

'It's all settled. Penny Maxwell, The Girl With The Golden Hands. Oh, very nice.' And nothing Penny could say would persuade him that she didn't really want that.

'How long shall I have to stay in London, then?' she asked.

He looked shrewdly at her.

'The terms of the competition are that you shall stay with us until our publicity campaign is launched,' he said, slowly. 'After all, it is well worth your while. The last campaign we ran like this resulted in the lucky girl being launched on a film career, and the one before that found a rich husband. Now you be a good girl and settle down to enjoy life. Lots of lovely clothes, and a tour of all the seaside resorts, should appeal to any pretty girl.'

Penny confided in Sylvie that night.

'I'm not very keen on all this,' she told her best friend.

Sylvie was quivering with excitement.

'Oh, if it were me, I'd just go ahead and do what they wanted me to. After all, it isn't going to be very hard, is it, just standing up and looking pretty, and saying a few things into a microphone? They even tell you what to say. And then you play that wonderful piano they've promised you. You ought to be very happy.'

'How about you, Sylvie?'

'Oh, I'm all right. Mike took me around London today, seeing the sights, and we went dancing this evening. He's fun.' She dragged herself back from her own happiness. 'I suppose you're thinking about that good-looking Paul Hambledon you told me about,' she guessed.

Penny flushed and looked away.

'Oh, I suppose he's forgotten all about me. Come to think of it, he never even knew where he could find me. I was just going to give him my address when that Audrey Bayfield came up and dragged him off to her car. I think he likes her a lot.'

'Well, this'll be a test,' Sylvie said suddenly and with enthusiasm. 'After all, your pictures will be in all the newspapers, so, when he sees them, he'll know where to get in touch. Everyone will see your pictures, all over the place.'

It was only too true. Someone saw Penny's picture — someone who was to change the course of Penny's destiny, and to bring her danger and excitement that even the Curly Corn Flakes Company couldn't bring her.

The girl who was looking at Penny's photograph was at that moment in a bed-sitting-room in a back street in London. Theatrical make-up and cos-tumes were scattered about and the girl was wearing too much make-up. But despite this, she was so much like Penny that they might have been twins.

Robina Trent stared at Penny's photograph unbelievingly at first, and then she leaned back, a shrewd, calculating look coming into the eyes that were so much like Penny's.

'I wonder,' she murmured to herself, her thoughts moving fast. 'I wonder — there might be something in this set-up for me.'

★　★　★

Robina Trent put the newspaper down, and sat back, thinking. It was too good an opportunity to miss. It wasn't every day that a girl came across her own double, and it was a red-letter day when that double had come into a slice of good fortune, such as this Penny Maxwell had.

Inside the newspaper was an interview with Penny. Robina read it avidly. Penny, the newspaper said, had a romantic background. There was a hint of mystery about her unknown family, and a whole lot about Penny's musical career. Some people, Robina decided, had all the luck.

She thought back over her own life, and envy stirred within her. Robina Trent had started life badly. She had been adopted by a woman who needed a companion for her own delicate little girl, who had died, leaving Robina, restless and difficult to remind her foster-mother constantly of the other child. Robina knew that she wasn't really loved, and had run away several times, but she had always been brought back.

When she left school her foster-mother had died, and Robina had got into bad company. Alone, with no one to advise her, she had chosen the easy way to make money, and found herself caught up with a bunch of crooks. Flash Farwell had been the leader and, although he hadn't treated her too badly. Robina had chafed at the lack of freedom, and the feeling that she always needed to look over her shoulder. One day, she promised herself, she would get free from Flash and his friends, and she would never again get tied up with people on the wrong side of the law. Now she had got free from them, and when she was in work she was constantly on the move, and her one-time friends couldn't keep up with her. But it was one thing to keep out of their way, by taking small part jobs in the theatre and moving about, but quite another thing to hope for a chance of glamour and easy money when she had to keep in the background all the time. Now that this girl, her double, had come into the picture, Robina thought she saw a way to alter all that. She must go and see this girl.

She got up and went through her wardrobe and settled at last on a plain corded silk two-piece, which suited her well. With it she wore a black pair of court shoes and carried a black suede handbag. A pink and grey hat sat perkily on her shining black hair, and her make-up was discreet for once.

But before she went briskly out of her

shabby little room, she felt drawn to look again at that picture of Penny Maxwell. It drew and held — it had a mysterious quality in that face, which made Robina suddenly shiver. She hesitated before setting out on what she was about to do, and almost decided to leave it alone. Then, with an angry shrug, she threw the newspaper down and walked out of the room.

Someone else was looking intently at that newspaper at the same time as Robina. It was Paul Hambledon.

He had bought the newspaper to read on the train. He had been to Elmdale, to visit Audrey Bayfield and her parents, only to learn that they were staying at a hotel in London so, as the day was free, he had caught the next train up to London and called on Audrey at the hotel.

Now, in the quiet West End hotel, Paul was left to wait for Audrey to come from her room, and he again turned to the newspaper, to read, with renewed amazement, of little Penny

Maxwell's good fortune. He was tremendously glad for Penny's sake, but he wondered if she was cut out for that sort of life. He hoped it wouldn't spoil her. He remembered her as the quiet type, and felt that she was too gentle and sweet to be put so suddenly into the limelight like that.

Andrey came downstairs at last. She was very angry with Paul for going off as he had done, leaving her for so long without any idea of what he was doing. She, too, had seen the publicity about Penny Maxwell and, into her jealous heart, sprang the suspicion that Paul had been with Penny in London all this time.

Paul sprang up when Audrey came into the lounge. She looked cool and lovely, and she had managed to hide her anger, and was smiling a welcome at him.

'Paul! I'm so glad to see you. Where have you been hiding yourself all this time? We've been anxious about you.'

'I've got myself a job,' he said,

laughing boyishly. 'I wasn't going to tell you all at first. Then I thought I might run down to Elmdale and look you all up, on my first free day from work, but I was told you were all up in London, so I thought I'd take a trip up here to see you.'

'But Paul, *you* working?' She pretended to be incredulous. 'What on earth are you *doing*, by way of a job?'

'Well, as a matter of fact, it's a publicity stunt,' he began.

Audrey's face clouded and her glance strayed to the newspaper he had put down when she came into the lounge.

'So that's where you've been!' she exclaimed. 'With *her*, all this time!'

His face registered the surprise he felt.

'Penny? Penny Maxwell? Don't be silly — my job's nothing to do with her. But it *is* grand news about her, isn't it?'

'I'm not interested in her,' Audrey said coldly, and then, feeling that she was making a mistake, since Paul had felt so kindly towards Penny Maxwell, she amended hastily. 'But of course, I'm terrifically glad for any girl in her position to get a bit of luck. It must be deadly to work in a cake-shop in a place like Elmdale.'

He smiled again.

'I thought you'd be pleased. She's such a nice little thing. I wondered if you'd seen her since I went away.'

'I've been away myself,' Audrey told him quickly, 'but you weren't interested enough to find that out, were you?'

'I'm sorry, Audrey,' he said, at once contrite. 'But there's so much to say and we haven't seen each other for so long. Where've you been? On holiday?'

'No, we've been to settle up the estate of an old great-uncle who just died up North. He had an emporium and he left it to me. I was his favourite niece.'

'Good heavens, what a thing to happen to you!' Paul said. 'So now you own an emporium in the North of England.'

'No. He lived up there but the

emporium is not too far away from home. In Sherwood Bay, as a matter of fact. It's called Wesley's.' She looked sharply at him. 'Why, what's wrong?'

His face showed his dismay.

'Oh, well, it's just the odd way things turn out, that's all,' he said at last. 'When I lost my money I never thought I'd ever have you as an employer, Audrey.'

She thought he was making fun of her.

'What do you mean, Paul?' she asked sharply. 'What if I do own Wesley's. It's quite a good emporium.'

'I know,' he said. 'That's what I mean. I work there.'

'No!' She was frankly astonished.

'That's what I was trying to tell you, when you jumped to the conclusion that I'd been with Penny Maxwell, in London. I hadn't. I've been working at Wesley's, in their music department. I expect you know all about the publicity stunt they've been doing, to get people interested in the music department. It was going down badly. Well, they run competitions, give away gramophone records, to people who can guess the names of the pieces being played. I'm the bloke who plays them.'

Audrey's eyes widened, and she started to laugh, with him. They both laughed, making a joke of it, to ease the tension. But Audrey didn't feel like laughing at jokes. She felt like shouting from the roof-tops with excitement at this new devepoment. She had been angry and bored at the thought of owning a department store and having to help to run it. But now that her newest employee was no less a person than Paul Hambledon, that made all the difference. All the difference in the world.

4

One of the biggest London parks stretched below the windows of the Splendide Hotel. Penny, who had got up that morning with a bad headache, looked wistfully out at the wide expanse of green, dotted with trees. Dogs scampered about and children played with balls or small boats. Penny longed to take a walk down there, in the air and the sunshine, but she had been instructed to stay in her room and wait for the car to come and whirl her off to the hairdresser, and then back to her room for a fitting for an evening gown.

And then her heart started to race as she saw someone she thought she knew, walking alone down there in the park. It was Paul Hambledon. Even at that distance he was unmistakable, with the proud set of his shoulders, and the careful way he held his head.

Without stopping to think Penny ran out of her room and down the corridor. The self-working lift was standing there, its doors invitingly open. She got it and sent it whirring down to the bottom wondering, as she waited for it to stop, whether Paul Hambledon would still be in sight and what he would say to her as she went running towards him.

By the time she had crossed the busy road, with its taxis and big private cars almost in one solid stream, Penny found that there was no sight of him. She hurried a little way in the direction he had been taking, but he had been swallowed up in the crowds of gay, happy people who dotted the grass.

Acutely disappointed, Penny sat down on a little green chair to regain her breath. Her headache came back with a renewed intensity and she began to consider telephoning Walter Wiley to ask if she could rest today and see the hairdresser and dressmaker tomorrow. At that moment, Mike and Sylvie came strolling across the grass.

Their faces lit up as they saw her.

'Penny! But you're supposed to be busy in your hotel, you said you weren't free today!' Sylvie cried.

Penny flushed. Not even to Sylvie, her best friend, could she bring herself to admit that she had been running after Paul Hambledon. Especially after Sylvie had said that now was the time for him to come and find Penny, if he really wanted to see her.

'The park looked so tempting from my windows,' she said lamely. 'And I've got a splitting headache.'

'Play truant!' Sylvie urged. 'Why shouldn't you — just for once! No one could blame you! The fun and the publicity is all right, but it's just plain boring to have to stay in the hotel a lovely day like this, just for old dressmaker fittings!'

'No, that isn't quite right, Sylvie,' Mike demurred. 'You mustn't say things like that to Penny. After all, she's got her part to play. I've been lucky. My part was taking the picture and collecting the prize. My time's my own from now on. But Penny's different. She's undertaken to do as they ask her to, in return for what she's getting.'

'Oh, I know, Mike,' Penny agreed. 'I wouldn't do anything like that. It's just that — oh, well, I'd better go back now.'

As she got up to go, Penny reeled a little.

'We'll go back with you,' Sylvie said firmly.

'No, I'm perfectly all right,' Penny told her. 'You know how I am when I get one of these heads, and it's always on a very bright, sunny day. Besides, the excitement, and all that. I'll lie down, with the blinds drawn, for a little while. Perhaps I'll be all right by the time the dressmaker comes. I can fix another appointment to have my hair done, I expect. But I must be fit and well for this afternoon's talent competition. I've got to play the piano and present the prizes.'

Sylvie and Mike reluctantly allowed

her to go back alone. After all, it was only across the road.

As always, with one of these bad headaches, Penny found that she was soon unable to focus properly. The bright sunlight on the coachwork of the sleek great cars that slid past her, blinded and dazzled her, as she waited at the edge of the kerb to cross.

One of the cars stopping by her seemed to be caught in the traffic block. Suddenly its back door was opened and a strong hand came out and pulled her inside. The traffic stream was moving more quickly now and, as the car slipped away from the kerb, Penny was held firmly on the back seat with a man's hand over her mouth.

It was all done quickly and smoothly so that the passers-by didn't even notice that anything was amiss. Penny couldn't shout for help and her head thudded painfully. A man's voice said in her ear; 'It's your own fault. You should have come back of your own free will.'

Penny felt that it was a nightmare.

Here she was, in broad daylight, kidnapped not many minutes after leaving Sylvie and Mike. For that was what it amounted to. She had been literally lifted off the pavement of a London street, into a car full of strange men, against her will.

She lay back and tried to think. After a while, the man took his hand away from her mouth, and started to talk to her.

'Don't let's have any more of this nonsense,' he told her gruffly but in a not unfriendly voice. 'I'm getting fed-up with you clearing off on your own, and wasting our time looking for you. You've worked well enough for us in the past. If you weren't so lazy and careless you'd get more out of it — a darn sight more than fooling about trying to get work on the stage.'

He waited, as if he expected her to speak. Penny was silent, her thoughts in a whirl. Obviously the man — all the men in the car, in fact — had mistaken her for someone else.

After a short silence he leaned back and lit a cigarette.

'All right,' he told Penny, 'if you mean to sulk it's okay by me. I'll leave you alone. You'll come to your senses later on, I expect.' And he turned to the man beside him and started talking in low tones.

Penny lay so quietly against the back seat that they seemed to take it for granted that she would make no more fuss. But out of her half-closed lids Penny was watching the busy London streets and, when the car was held up by traffic lights, Penny suddenly grabbed the car door and wrenched it open. A policeman, who had been watching the traffic getting entangled on the far side of the crossroads, moved over in that direction. He hadn't noticed Penny tumble out of the car. But the fact that he had been there had stopped the men from attempting to go after her.

She plunged into the middle of a crowd of people crossing the road and, because she had no handbag with her and couldn't buy a bus ticket, she hurried with the stream of people, until she saw a cruising taxi, and hailed it.

The incident had left her white and shaken. When she got back to the hotel she asked the commissionaire to pay the cab off, and stumbled up the steps.

The receptionist came quickly from behind the desk.

'My dear, aren't you well?' she asked.

'It's the sun, my head's thumping,' Penny stammered.

'I'll get someone to see you up to your room,' the receptionist said.

'Oh, no thank you, I'll just lie down for a little while,' Penny said.

All that Penny wanted was to be alone, to think over the terrifying thing that had just happened to her.

But no sooner had she pulled her curtains and flopped down on her bed than she was disturbed again by the house phone. Someone, the receptionist said, had called to see her.

Wearily Penny answered. 'Who is it?'

'She says her name is Miss Robina Trent.'

Penny's heart sank. Walter Wiley had warned her that a lot of people, complete strangers, would want to talk to her, and he had hinted that as she was now in the public eye, she must not refuse to see them.

'All right. Will you send her up, please?' Penny asked the receptionist.

There was a knock on the door a little later. Penny went to open it. A girl of her own height and build stood there and, as Penny looked at her, the girl took off her sun glasses and smiled.

Penny fell back a step with astonishment. After the episode of the attempted kidnapping she wondered if the sun had made her light-headed: for, looking at this girl who stood outside her hotel room door, was like looking in the mirror at her own self.

After a long moment, Penny found her voice.

'Won't you come in?' she gasped.

Robina Trent smiled sweetly.

'I hope you won't think it an awful cheek on my part. I am a perfect stranger to you; but, honestly, when I saw your picture in the papers, I just couldn't believe my eyes. I *had* to come and see you!'

Penny shook her head in bewilderment.

'You're exactly like me,' she gasped.

'I know,' Robina laughed. 'It's a queer feeling, isn't it, seeing someone who looks exactly like yourself?'

Penny's head was thumping but this new situation was one she couldn't put off for another day. She turned round and looked in the mirror, and Robina came and stood beside her. It really was uncanny.

'We might almost pass as twins,' Robina remarked cheerfully.

Penny turned to her.

'Tell me about yourself. Have you got any sisters?'

Robina shook her head.

'No one at all. I'm an orphan — brought up in an orphanage, in fact, until I was adopted. How about you?'

'But how strange!' Penny gasped. 'That's exactly what happened to me! What do you do for a living? I work in a shop.'

'I'm on the stage.' Robina pulled a face. 'It's a hard life, but it's interesting. I can't do anything else, anyway. But I'm 'resting' at the moment.'

'Look, we mustn't lose touch with each other,' Penny said, impulsively. Robina, at her most charming, was very hard to resist, and Penny saw nothing of the real Robina underneath, the ruthless Robina who would seize any chance to further her own ends.

'I hoped you'd say that,' Robina admitted. 'You see, I could be of help to you. If you've only worked in a shop, you may find this business of appearing in public rather strange, whereas I'm used to it. I could give you a few tips, if you like.'

A wave of nausea came over Penny and she whitened.

'I say, aren't you well? You look a bit

queer,' Robina said, quickly.

'Migraine,' Penny muttered. 'I woke up with it. And I went out to get a breath of fresh air, and the most awful thing happened to me.' She hesitated but Robina's inviting air was persuasive, and Penny decided to tell the other girl about the kidnapping. It would be a relief to tell someone.

Robina listened with a sympathetic expression on her face, but a new wariness in her eyes. A little thrill of apprehension shot through her as she listened. So they were after her again, Flash Farwell and his friends! It was an odd streak of chance that they had mistaken Penny Maxwell for Robina herself, but it was a warning to Robina. She had got away from them once, and she didn't intend to go back again!

As Penny paused, Robina said:

'What an awful experience for you. What will you do about it?'

'I don't know. I ought to go and tell the Publicity Manager about it, I suppose. But all I want to do at the moment is to crawl into bed and forget everything. Oh, I forgot! I can't do that, though. I've got to judge a talent competition this afternoon and play the piano.'

'But you can't go, feeling like that!' Robina protested. 'Can't you telephone the Curly Corn Flakes people and cancel it?'

'Oh, no, I couldn't do that!' Penny said, distractedly. 'It's a very tight programme and, anyway, it would be too short notice to cancel it.'

'Can I help?' Robina murmured, controlling her excitement at the thought of taking Penny's place. 'I mean, if you put it to them, explained everything, they'd agree all right! I've often understudied. It's easy for me, and it would solve everything for them and for you, and no one need be disappointed. What do you say?'

Penny was overcome with gratitude.

'Oh, would you? Would you do it for me?'

'If I can,' Robina said, slowly. 'I mean, if you think it would be all right. I'm quite willing.'

And so Penny agreed to let Robina take her place. She didn't realise, in making that decision, how she was altering the future, not only of herself, but of many people around her.

They compared notes. Robina could play the piano. Her voice was very much like Penny's too. And their personal measurements were almost exact. There seemed to be nothing to interfere with the plan and Penny was happy and relieved that, in this emergency, she wouldn't be letting down the Curly Corn Flakes organisation.

'Look, I'll tell you what we'll do,' Robina said. 'I'll change into the clothes you have to wear for this afternoon, then I won't have to come back and disturb you. I'll go downstairs and telephone your Mr. Wiley and tell him what we've arranged between us, then if he doesn't object, I can go straight to the Curly Corn Flakes factory.'

'No, the arrangement was to have lunch at Sambrini's first,' Penny explained quickly. 'One of their people will be waiting for you there. After lunch, he'll take you in the car to the Curly Corn Flakes factory.'

'All right, then. If your Mr. Wiley agrees on the telephone, I'll take a cab there. Just time,' Robina agreed.

Penny, who was only too anxious to lie down with a couple of aspirin tablets and go to sleep, helped Robina to put on the outfit for the afternoon's talent concert.

Robina twirled round in the smart outfit Penny was to have worn.

'How do I look?' she asked and then, flinging out her hands and smiling to an imaginary audience just beyond Penny's shoulder, she began, 'Ladies and gentlemen, it gives me great pleasure — ' and broke off, laughing at Penny's expression.

'You see?' Robina laughed. 'When

you're used to it, there's nothing in it!'

'I couldn't do it like that,' Penny confessed.

Robina, acting the part of the warm and sympathetic friend, tucked Penny into bed and made her feel that there was nothing to worry about at all. This girl, who had appeared from nowhere, and who looked so uncannily like herself, was a real friend, and would see to everything.

She listened to Robina's footsteps going confidently down the corridor, and let her eyelids droop, only too willing to sink into oblivion for a few hours, and lose the nagging pain.

But Robina had no intention of telephoning Walter Wiley, or of explaining about the impersonation. Instead, she meant to go there as Penny Maxwell.

She stepped out of the lift with the spark of excitement in her eyes, and saw a good-looking young man talking to the clerk at the reception desk. It was the relief clerk, who took over for the lunch hour, so she hadn't seen Robina go up to Penny's room, and she didn't know that Penny was unwell. She took it for granted that this was the pretty girl who had won the competition.

'Oh, there you are, Miss Maxwell,' she smiled. 'Here is a visitor for you — I was just going to telephone up to you.'

Paul Hambledon came forward.

'Penny!' he exclaimed. 'I've just seen your photograph in the newspaper and I've come to congratulate you on your good fortune.'

Robina smiled briefly. This was going to be tricky. The newspapers had said that Penny Maxwell was completely unattached, but here was a man friend who was difficult to place.

He looked just the type she herself would be interested in, but something wasn't quite right about him, in Robina's opinion. He looked as if he might be well-off, to judge by his manner, and yet he was very carelessly dressed. She decided to try him out.

'I was just going to a lunch appointment before going to the Curly Corn Flakes factory for my afternoon engagement,' she said, slowly. 'You can run me there, if you like.'

'But you know I haven't got my car any longer, Penny,' Paul Hambledon reminded her with a frown. Something, he considered, was different about Penny and he hoped that her sudden success hadn't gone to her head.

'Oh, I forgot,' Robina said, hastily. 'Never mind, I'll manage. I'll take a cab.' If the young man hadn't a car any longer, it suggested that he hadn't much money, so he wasn't going to be any use to her, Robina decided.

Paul Hambledon was stung by her cool tone and her words. 'I see,' he said, quietly. 'I'm sorry to have troubled you, Penny. I can quite understand how you feel. I've lost all my money and you're on the high tide of success. Well, good luck, anyway,' he said, as he swung on his heel and left the hotel.

5

Robina was enjoying herself deputising for Penny.

She had taken a taxi to Sambrini's and found to her delight that the young man from the Curly Corn Flakes company was also a stranger to Penny, so that overcame the first snag. He introduced himself.

'I'm Peter Norton, Mr. Wiley's assistant,' he said, and it struck Robina that he wasn't very keen on being the one assigned to take Penny to lunch.

His manner was doubtful, as if he thought it was going to be hard work keeping Penny entertained.

Robina, mischief in her eyes, set out to be as alluring as she could and, before the lunch was over, the young man had become quite infatuated with her.

He delivered her into Walter Wiley's

hands with regret and, as soon as he had an opportunity of speaking to his chief, he said, in a surprised voice:

'I didn't find her at all reserved or shy as you said she would be. She's marvellous!'

Walter Wiley was surprised to hear Peter talk like this. He had found her very shy during his publicity campaign with her. He would have been even more surprised had he known that the girl with whom his assistant had lunched was not Penny Maxwell at all.

Robina had a further surprise in store for Walter Wiley. She walked with assurance on to the stage at Curly Corn Flakes' model factory, and smiled winningly at the audience, who gave an instant and spontaneous applause, before Walter Wiley had a chance to speak.

'Our lovely competition winner has ambitions,' he went on, after introducing her, smiling first at the audience and then at the row of young employees who were entering for a talent competition. 'She wants a musical career. Well, here's the piano. Let's see what she can do before she sees what we can do!'

He looked kindly at the girl he took to be Penny, but was surprised to find that she didn't seem to be in the least bit nervous.

Robina knew that Penny played classical music, but that wasn't her own strong point, so she took charge of the situation at once.

'Oh, this is a gala occasion!' she told the audience, laughing infectiously. 'You don't want me to show off. I tell you what I'll do — I'll give you a medley and anything you recognise, join in and sing your heads off!'

That appealed to the audience and she had them warmed up right away. There was a good deal of fun and laughter as she flicked in and out of first one well-known song and then another. Robina gave them their money's worth in the time allotted to her. It was a surprised Walter Wiley who came out on to the stage again, to take charge of the proceedings, and to introduce the competition entrants.

By the time it came to the judging and the presenting of the prizes he was completely staggered.

'What did I tell you?' Peter Norton said. 'This girl's no shy violet — she's got something!'

Walter Wiley watched Robina presenting the prizes, with a thoughtful air. To everyone who came up to her she had something to say which brought a grateful smile, or a laugh, in which the audience joined. They were all thoroughly enjoying themselves.

'That wasn't what I expected of our Penny Maxwell at all!' he half murmured to Peter Norton. 'I'm knocked for six! If that's what she can do, we'll really go places over this campaign!'

★ ★ ★

Paul Hambledon was bitterly disappointed as he left the Splendide Hotel.

He hadn't believed it possible that Penny Maxwell could be so changed in such a short time, or that her head could really be turned by all the adulation she was getting.

Shrugging, he called at Audrey's hotel to see if she would be free for lunch. She was — and she accepted his invitation readily.

After lunch he asked her what she would like to do.

'Oh, Paul, darling, I've got a wonderful idea,' she said. 'Daddy has shares in the Curly Corn Flakes company. It would be a simple matter to get good seats in the front row at the talent competition at the factory this afternoon. Daddy has shares in most things,' she finished, laughing at Paul's look of surprise. 'Come on, let's go and see what she makes of it. You know you want to.'

She waited, with bated breath, hoping he would say he wasn't interested in Penny Maxwell, and yet unable to resist the urge to go and see what Penny would be like on the stage. She was secretly hoping that Penny would make a mess of it all. Anything to discredit Penny in Paul's eyes. He must be made to forget Penny Maxwell — or be ashamed to remember her!

Paul relucantly agreed because to refuse would have been discourteous.

Audrey made a quick telephone call, and announced that it would be all right.

'Personally I just can't imagine what she'll do, after being in a shop all her life, and with no training for this sort of thing,' Audrey said, with a superior smile, as she drove them both to the Curly Corn Flakes factory.

The two front rows were occupied by the important people concerned with the company and the publicity campaign. Audrey and Paul were in full view of the stage, and Paul wondered uneasily if it would make Penny nervous when she saw them. She wouldn't be able to avoid spotting them, he decided.

When the curtains swept back, and Walter Wiley led on the girl in the model frock and wicked little hat, Paul stared in astonishment, and even Audrey lifted her eyebrows in surprise. It was indeed difficult to believe that this smiling, self-confident, alluring creature, who evoked prompt applause from the packed audience, was the rather reserved girl from Elmdale.

Audrey stole a glance at Paul, to see his reactions but, as time wore on, and the girl they believed to be Penny carried the audience with her performance and competently presented prizes for the amateur talent, Paul looked more and more puzzled.

'What's the matter?' Audrey whispered.

'Well, I thought she'd be all right,' Paul answered slowly, 'but not like this! This is, well, a professional performance, don't you think?'

Audrey shrugged, annoyed.

'I think she's making an exhibition of herself, if that's what you mean!' she said sharply. 'Walter Wiley's making it all rather easy for her, anyway.'

She said she wanted to leave early, as she had an evening date, so Paul took her out to her car.

As they left the factory Paul said slowly:

'It's odd, but I keep feeling that the girl we've been watching *isn't* Penny Maxwell at all.'

Audrey was astonished.

'Paul, what a silly thing to say! Of course it's Penny Maxwell — who else could it be?'

'I don't know,' he said slowly, unaware of the mounting flush of annoyance on Audrey's face, as she looked straight ahead. 'It's a peculiar feeling I got, when I was watching her up there on the stage. Little things, the inflexion of the voice, the way she pronounces a word here and there, just a little different from the way Penny does it. That girl was terribly *like* Penny and yet, as you say, who else could it be, if it isn't Penny?'

'I think you're being absurd,' Audrey said, irritably. 'Really, Paul, since the sale of your old home, and the time when you met that girl, you haven't been the same.'

'Am I different, Audrey?'

'Yes, you are — and different in a way that I don't care for, Paul. You used to be the ideal companion. You used to like the same things as I did. And now, all you can talk about is that girl. Penny Maxwell! I'm tired of the sound of her name!'

'Are you?' he said, slowly. 'But I like her. Don't you like her, Audrey?'

She pulled up at the traffic lights and, in the short pause, she turned to stare at him, in almost hostile fashion.

'Are you mad, Paul? Why should I like her? We haven't anything in common. She just isn't in our world. We're poles apart. She means nothing to me. And, frankly, I can't see what on earth she could mean to you, either.'

'Isn't that for me to say?' he asked, quietly.

She whitened but, as the lights changed, she had to give her attention to the driving. When they spoke again it was on another subject entirely. But Audrey knew that in Penny Maxwell she had a formidable rival.

* * *

When Robina came back to the Splendide Hotel that evening she was flushed with triumph and excitement. Penny, who had managed to sleep most of the day, staggered out of her bed to open the door for her.

Robina composed her face. She didn't want Penny to think she had enjoyed herself too much.

'How are you?' she asked Penny, sympathetically.

'Oh, a lot better, I think,' Penny said, weakly. 'My headache's eased up, but I feel rather queer. How did the show go?'

'Everything went fine.' Robina frowned. 'Have you had anything to eat since I left you?'

Penny looked surprised.

'No, as a matter of fact, I haven't. I've been sleeping.'

'I'll ring down for something at once,' Robina decided. 'Something light. Let's see, some tea and thin bread and butter, and a lightly boiled egg. Oh, and some fruit or jelly if they can rustle up some. How does that sound?'

'You're awfully kind,' Penny said, gratefully.

'Look here,' Robina said slowly, after she had phoned down for her light meal, 'it was all right today, me taking your place, I mean. But naturally, it won't have to get about that there are two of us. Maybe I'd better keep out of the way.'

'Well, there isn't anything to hide, is there?' Penny objected, looking anxious.

'Don't be silly,' Robina laughed. 'This isn't your show, or mine, come to that. It's a publicity stunt run by a big company. It might ruin everything if the public found out that there were two girls, and they never knew which one they were being shown. Do you see what I mean?'

'Oh, yes, I see your point,' Penny agreed. 'Well, how shall we manage it? You won't want the hotel people to know, either, will you?'

'Well, that won't come into it much,' Robina pointed out, 'because there's been a change of plans. They want you to pack tomorrow and leave this hotel, so that they can start the seaside tour sooner than they intended. Think you can manage it, or would you like me to help you pack?'

'I think I can manage,' Penny said, but she looked dismayed. Robina could see that she was still far from well.

'I think I'd better go back to my lodgings as soon as you've had your meal. It'll be busy downstairs and the night receptionist will be on duty,' Robina said.

There was a knock on the door and Robina signed to Penny to answer it, while she slipped into the private bathroom. The trolley of supper was wheeled in. When Penny was alone again, Robina came out of the bathroom.

Penny sank into a nearby chair.

'What's the matter?' Robina asked sharply.

'I — I'm not sure if I shall be able to leave here tomorrow,' Penny faltered. 'I feel so peculiar. Do you think I'm going to be ill?'

Robina felt Penny's forehead.

'You're rather hot. I think you've got a temperature. Probably a chill. Or maybe it's nerves. I suppose you've been letting all this excitement get you down.'

'Couldn't you go instead of me, as you're free at the moment?' Penny pleaded. 'As Mr. Wiley knows about us it can't matter much, can it?'

Robina shot Penny a sharp look. Penny had not asked very much about this afternoon, which indicated that she was far from well, and Robina had no intention of disclosing that Walter Wiley didn't know anything about the switch of girls.

It was a tempting situation and Robina felt excitement rising at the thought of being able to carry on in Penny's place. This was more than she had hoped for.

'I don't mind helping you out a bit,' she said, slowly, 'provided nothing turns up for me from the theatrical agency.'

'Oh, I'd be so grateful if you would,' Penny said, 'but of course you mustn't lose any chances yourself, where your own work's concerned. I only need a day or two, I'm sure.'

'Well, let's think this thing out,' Robina said. 'You'll have to leave this hotel, you know. After all, you can't expect the Curly Corn Flakes company to go on paying for you here. I think the best thing would be for you to go and lay up at my place.'

Penny looked apprehensive, but Robina assured her.

'It's not much of a place after this I admit, but my landlady's marvellous when anyone isn't well. She'll look after you. And I'll carry on for you till you get in touch with me. But if anything turns up for me you will let me know at once, won't you?'

Penny promised she would.

'I'll leave you the addresses and times we'll be there, as Walter Wiley gave them to me,' Robina said, writing them down. 'There. Now I'll get a taxi for you.'

She looked critically at Penny.

'You'll have to go by yourself, I'm afraid, if we don't want everyone catching on that there are two of us. Do you think you can manage to get down to the street? After that, you'll be all right. It won't take long to my door.'

Penny said she thought she could manage it. She seemed only too grateful to have someone shift the burden of responsibility from her shoulders.

'It'll be better to go tonight, I think,' Robina comforted her. 'I'll stay here, in your place. You needn't get up in the morning then. Ma Addy's a good sort about breakfast in bed, when you're not up to much.'

'But what about the packing?' Penny gasped.

'Oh, don't worry about that,' Robina assured her. 'I'll see to that. The Corn Flakes people will settle the bill and Peter Norton, the one I met today, is coming to pick me up and drive me down to the first coast town they're going to do.'

Robina got together Penny's few personal things and helped Penny into the clothes she herself had worn to come to the hotel in. Acting a part, she seemed to Penny to be kindness itself, and Penny wondered how she could have managed without her timely help.

She sat on the edge of the bed and listened to Robina efficiently arranging with the cab rank on the telephone for a taxi to take a young lady to No. 7 Marguerita Street which, as she explained to Penny afterwards, was a little street off a thriving market, just two districts away.

Penny hardly remembered how she got down to the street. The hotel was filled and busy. She had a dim recollection of brilliant lights and people milling about, but no one took any notice of her. She was thankful when the driver got out of his cab and helped her into the back seat.

The journey was a dream. At last he said:

'Here we are, miss,' and he told her how much the fare came to. Penny paid him, and walked uncertainly towards the narrow flight of whitened steps up to the little house where Robina lodged.

6

Sylvie and Mike had their long week-end in London but, when the time came for them to return to Elmdale, they felt they had to see Penny again.

'Let's just make a flying visit,' Sylvie urged. 'No matter how busy Penny is she'll manage a little while with us, I know!'

'Wait a bit,' Mike objected. 'We'd better phone first and find out if it's convenient.'

They found a telephone box and squeezed in together. Mike left the telephoning to Sylvie but, when she got through and started speaking, he saw her frown in a puzzled way.

'Is that Penny?' she asked.

It was Robina who answered. She was busy packing and was annoyed at being interrupted.

'Who is speaking?' she asked, rather sharply.

'It's Sylvie,' came the reply. 'Penny, are you all right? Is your head still bad?'

Robina thought quickly. Some more friends of Penny's that she hadn't been warned about!

'Yes, I got rid of that all right yesterday,' she said shortly. 'Look, I'm in a bit of a rush at the moment. Packing to start the publicity tour. D'you mind if I don't talk now?'

Sylvie, flushing a little, said:

'Well, we only wanted to know if you could see us for a minute, as we're going back to Elmdale.'

Mike took the telephone from her and was going to say a few words himself when he heard Robina answering.

'Can't you say good-bye now, over the telephone? I really am in the most awful rush.'

'Don't worry,' Mike said into the receiver. 'We know you're busy, Penny. Let us know how you get on, won't you?'

Robina didn't know that this was the young man who had taken that so-important photograph which won the competition.

'Who's that speaking?' she asked sharply.

Mike stared blankly at the receiver and then at Sylvie.

'It's Mike,' he said slowly.

Robina knew by the tone of his voice that she had made a slip.

'Look,' she said, desperately, trying to put things right, 'I'm sorry if I sound a bit short, but I really am in a rush just now. The car will be here for me in a minute, and I'm not half ready. I'll get in touch with you the moment I have a chance.'

'Don't worry,' Mike said in a hurt voice. 'It's nothing. We just thought we'd like to say good-bye. Best of luck, Penny,' and he hung up.

Sylvie had heard most of the conversation; Robina's clear voice carried, and Sylvie, too, had been surprised.

'Perhaps she's got someone with her, and it was a bit awkward, taking a private call,' she said, tucking her arm into Mike's as they left the call box.

'Yes, but her voice sounded different,' Mike objected.

'It wasn't like her to answer so sharply,' Sylvie agreed, 'but I bet she'll be miserable about it until she can get in touch with us and explain.'

But Penny's condition at that moment was much more than miserable.

She had managed to get up the stairs but the landlady, who had watched her coming in, had followed her, obviously bewildered as to what was the matter with her. Penny paused at the head of the stairs, faced with a row of doors. Robina had forgotten to tell her which was her door.

'What's the matter, ducks?' the landlady asked. 'You look real queer.'

'Oh, I'll be all right,' Penny said quickly, holding on to the banisters.

'But it must be something!' Mrs. Addy objected. 'You were all right when you went out this morning. You must be in a state if you don't know your own room! Here, I'll open your door for you.'

She went to the middle door and, opening it, she switched on the light and stood aside for Penny to go in.

Penny looked inside the room and her heart sank.

Was she to stay in this room, with its clothes all over the place, the smell of greasepaint and perfume strong in the air?

She went in and, despite her feeling so ill, she remembered to be careful in the way she answered.

'I had a fierce headache; it must be the sun.'

'Headache from the sun? *You?*' Mrs. Addy laughed. 'I've never known you to have anything like that before!'

She waited expectantly and Penny hoped she would go, before she suspected anything. She seemed to know Robina very well.

'Well, come on, ducks,' Mrs. Addy

encouraged. 'How did it go off?'

'What?' Penny asked, bewildered.

'The audition, of course! I watched you go off, and looking real nice you was, too, and if I may so. Ever so excited you looked and I could hardly wait till you got back. I didn't expect you looking like this, I must say!'

'I don't know how it went off,' Penny said, truthfully. 'To tell you the truth, I think I've got a chill.'

'Oh, well now, that's different,' Mrs. Addy said. 'A chill I can understand and deal with. That might happen to anyone. Into bed with you, my girl, and I'll bring you up hot water bottles and some hot milk. We'll get you on your feet again in no time.'

She was as good as her word and did everything she could for Penny.

But Penny didn't respond to Mrs. Addy's treatment and, at last, the landlady decided she'd have to call in the doctor.

'Goodness knows,' Mrs. Addy clucked. 'When the doctor will get here, poor fella, that run off his feet, he is.'

'I'll be all right,' Penny insisted feebly.

'Of course you will, dearie,' Mrs. Addy said, comfortingly, plumping up her pillows and straightening the bed.

Penny closed her eyes and heard Mrs. Addy go out. She listened to her going down the stairs, and she must have dozed. Voices outside on the landing woke her up.

'She's ill, all right. Lost the sharp tone in her voice, and actually grateful, instead of high-and-mighty, for once,' Mrs. Addy was saying. 'Not that I can help myself, whatever she's like to me, with that pretty face of hers.'

She started to go downstairs, and Penny heard a man's voice answer her.

'It's only because of being on the stage, mum. They all get a bit hard-boiled. They can't help it. She isn't like that underneath, I know she isn't.'

'Oh, go on with you, Joe! You always

have been silly over her, but you get worse.'

'Gosh, I wish that doctor'd hurry up,' the young man answered. 'Did you tell him it was urgent?'

'That I did!' Mrs. Addy said stoutly, almost at the bottom of the stairs. 'Aye, and here he is now.'

She came puffing upstairs again, this time with the doctor, an elderly man with kindly, twinkling eyes. He examined Penny, and asked her questions.

'Nothing organically wrong. Something upset you lately? Scared you, maybe?' he asked.

With Mrs. Addy in the room, Penny felt she could hardly tell him that she had almost been kidnapped. But she did admit that she had had a shock, and told him about the headache.

'Bed's the best place for you, for the next two or three days,' he pronounced, writing a prescription. 'Take these tablets as prescribed and you needn't call me in again unless you're no better.

Perfect rest and quiet should put you right.'

With a cheerful nod, he left Penny.

Mrs. Addy was kindness itself, but Penny heard no more of Joe.

Most of the day she slept, and the doctor's tablets did her a lot of good. When she woke on the third morning she felt more like her old self than she had done since she left Elmdale.

There was a gentle knock on the door and, thinking it was Mrs. Addy, Penny called; 'Come in.'

A young man in shirt sleeves opened the door, pushing it wide with his back as he carried a tray nicely laid with a light breakfast and a pot of tea.

He was lean and wiry, with flaxen hair that tended to curl, and his face crinkled with laughter creases. His honest brown eyes reminded Penny of Mrs. Addy and she guessed that this was the kindly landlady's son, Joe.

'Mum said I could bring your breakfast up this morning, Robina. How are you?' he asked, putting the tray on the table by the bed and turning to Penny.

His smile faded as he looked down at her. Penny was one of those lucky people who look nice when they first wake up. She had no make-up on and her lovely little face was flushed from sleep, like a baby's. She showed little or no traces of her brief illness but she was very embarrassed at being caught in bed like this by a strange young man who obviously thought she was Robina.

'That's very kind of you,' Penny said, avoiding his eyes. 'I'm feeling much better, thank you.'

He was silent. Penny didn't know that Robina was always impatient with him, even rude at times. In fact, she had never even heard of Joe Addy and his obvious interest in Robina, before she had come here, and angrily told herself that Robina might have warned her.

'You don't have to put on all that politeness for me, Robina,' Joe said at last, in a hurt voice. 'I think I'd rather you were rude to me as you usually are.'

Penny was distressed. She didn't know what to say.

Making the best of a difficult situation, she said slowly; 'I'm — I don't know what to say, about all this kindness from you and your mother. I don't know why you should both be so kind to me,' and, indeed, she meant it, feeling more acutely than before, how much a total stranger to them she was.

'You know why I'm kind to you, Robina,' Joe said huskily. 'As to mum, why, she can't help it. She's kind to everyone, you know that. But if she doesn't understand you sometimes I must say you've only got yourself to blame. You don't have to be so sharp with her, do you?'

Penny flushed. Why was Robina so thoughtless and offhanded to these good people?

'Here, I'll get your bed-jacket,' Joe said, opening a cupboard with a natural manner which suggested that he was used to waiting on Robina. Penny couldn't resent the action and he put the jacket round her shoulders with a gentleness that brought a lump to her throat.

'There,' he said, 'eat your breakfast and forget what I said. You know I wouldn't say a cross word to you, if I could help it.'

Penny watched him go out and softly shut the door behind him. How was it going to end, this business of the two of them stepping into each other's shoes? If she herself was doing the right thing at Robina's end, what was Robina doing at her end?

Hand to her mouth with dismay, Penny thought over this new angle of the situation. And then she told herself not to be a fool. There was no need to worry about her own end. She had no complications. Paul Hambledon hadn't bothered to get into touch with her, she reminded herself, so there was no need to worry about what Robina would say to him.

But how wrong she was!

Paul Hambledon was very miserable about Penny. He would keep away from her, he told himself, if that was what she wanted. She was doing very well for herself and, in all fairness, he asked himself why she should be interested in him.

He went back to Sherwood Bay, to his job at the emporium, but his heart wasn't in his work.

Holidaymakers swarmed to the little town in their thousands, because of the new excursion rates of the trains, and the new coach tours that were including Sherwood Bay in their list of stopping places. Someone with money was doing his best to put the little town on the map and, before Paul's day off, he had felt the excitement of it all.

He sat in the big window of the music department, playing the piano, which drew the crowds.

Sometimes he improvised, and he

had composed a little tune which people were beginning to ask about.

'What's is called?' a pert redhead in the crowd had asked him one day.

On impulse, Paul had said: 'The Girl With The Raven-Black Hair.'

He was thinking of Penny at the time. It was before his visit to London. The crowd started to hum the tune.

On the day after he returned from London, Paul was surprised to find his immediate chief waiting for him.

'Look here, that new tune you play, Hambledon,' he began. 'People are asking about it. Have you got the words?'

Paul shook his head.

'No, sir, it's just a tune that I composed as I went along. Someone asked me what it was called and — well, I'm afraid I made the title up on the spur of the moment.'

'Can you write some words?' the manager asked energetically. 'It's caught their imagination.'

But Paul's enthusiasm had gone. The

title and the tune merely irritated him now.

'Oh, why don't they write the words if they're so mad keen on it?' he exploded.

The manager didn't take offence. He saw possibilities in young Paul Hambledon. Instead he said:

'It's an idea at that! Yes, young fellow, I think you've got something there! Let me see. A competition, supplying lyrics to the tune. You can help with the judging as you are the composer.'

And so a new competition was launched in Sherwood Bay. The prizes were tempting and the emporium, under its new paint, and its startling hoardings, drew more crowds than it had ever done in the old days, when Audrey's old great-uncle, Wesley, had owned it.

It was a tremendous success, that competition, and Paul, on impulse, felt that Penny ought to know about it. She probably did already, he reminded himself since, according to the hoardings on the pierhead and the station, the Curly Corn Flakes campaign had reached Redsands, further along the coast. He felt it would be a good excuse for him to go and see her.

Redsands was a new and modern town. It had a picture-postcard look. Yellow sands, white cliffs and green turf on top, smart hotels and shops, a pier and a boating pool. And a wonderful pavilion, where Penny's white piano graced the flower-banked stage.

Again Paul sat in the front row, and watched the girl he took to be Penny, perform. Walter Wiley seemed to be enjoying himself now, as he brought her out by the hand and introduced her, and again the audience took her to their hearts.

Robina, in Penny's wonderful new clothes, certainly was good to look at.

After the show, Paul sent a note round to the back, asking if he might see Penny alone for a few minutes. He was taken to her dressing-room, but there were crowds there. It was like a West End show. Walter Wiley was there, and everyone was praising Robina and wanting to speak to her.

Paul had a struggle to get near her but, when he did, he was shocked to find that the brilliant smile wavered for a second, as she caught sight of him. It was there again in a minute, but Paul had been quick to see the shadow over her face. She didn't want to see him!

'Penny. I've got to see you alone,' he managed to whisper.

Robina frowned. This young man was going to be a nuisance. She hadn't expected him to turn up here. She had a wealthy playboy and two or three other interesting men lined up and dating her as fast as they could. She didn't want any of them to think that there was someone who had a prior claim on her time and company.

'Later,' she said and then, thinking quickly, she added, 'Ring me, at this number, when I leave the show.'

Paul found himself edged out of her

immediate circle by the press of other people.

In his hand was a card, with the name of the hotel and her telephone number.

He had half a mind not to call her up, but the urge to speak to her was too strong. He waited, and saw her go out to her car, still surrounded by crowds of admirers, and with Walter Wiley in close attendance. Paul gave her time to get to her hotel and then telephoned.

When she came on the line her voice had the suggestion of a hard note in it, and she said, 'Who is speaking?'

'It's Paul. Don't you recognise my voice? I hope I've given you time enough to speak to me, Penny.'

Robina thought quickly. She would have to use different tactics with this young man.

'Look,' she said, toning down the harsh note in her voice. 'Let's be sensible about this. You know what this tour means to me and you know that I have to do practically as I'm told. It isn't my wish not to see my old friends, but there it is.'

Paul, after a shocked silence, said quietly: 'I see.'

'No, you don't,' she said, turning on the charm belatedly. It wouldn't do to rob poor Penny of all her friends, Robina supposed. That wasn't her intention, but merely to keep them from spoiling her own chances!

'All I want — all I am suggesting is, let's wait till the tour's over, and I can do as I like again. What do you say?'

'I'll do more than that, Penny,' Paul said quietly. 'I'll leave you alone altogether. I've been very dense, but at last I can see that's what you want. Don't bother to let me down lightly. I can take a hint.'

He rang off, his disappointment so keen that he had forgotten all about the song.

But Robina was left staring angrily at the telephone. That wasn't what she had wanted at all. She was used to being high-handed with young men, but they usually kept coming back, and rarely took offence like this. It was she who made the running, not them! Besides, it was her rule in life never to burn her boats. One never knew whom one would need to fall back on, at some time or other, and this young man appeared to be the steady, reliable type.

7

Mike went back to his studio in his aunt's shop and found that in Elmdale he was an important person now.

'It's nice to see you back,' Miss Bailey said, with a welcoming hug. 'Just a matter of a few days you've been away, Mike, my love, and you should just see the sittings I've fixed for you! Well, I've had to go out and buy a smart book to enter them!'

Mike stared at the book she proudly offered to him, and saw the amount of work which had accumulated. He whistled softly.

'Pleased, eh?' she beamed at him. 'The tide's turned, Mike, and all due to our little Penny. And now, tell me all about her while I just brew this pot of tea.'

Mike sat down to an appetising meal

and told his aunt about all that had happened.

'And then Penny seemed to change,' he finished doubtfully. 'Oh, don't ask me how! I just don't know. Her voice sounded a bit different and she wouldn't see us to say goodbye. Sylvie was rather hurt about it, and I didn't like it much myself.'

'Perhaps she was still a bit under the weather,' Miss Bailey said comfortingly. 'I've known her to have one of those headaches for days. Sensitive girl, Penny, easily upset, though she mightn't show it.'

But the next morning Miss Bailey, fetching in the newspapers and magazines, gave Mike his at the breakfast table and said thoughtfully:

'Funny you should say that about Penny, Mike.'

'Why?' he asked.

She had her favourite weekly in her hand, and in it was an illustrated article about competition winners, Penny in particular. Miss Bailey stared down at a picture of Robina at the Pavilion at Redsands. Robina standing at the edge of the stage, her arms flung outwards, a wide, all-embracing smile on her face, completely at home up there behind the footlights.

'If I didn't think it'd sound so silly,' Miss Bailey said slowly, 'I'd almost say that wasn't our Penny.'

Mike got up and looked over her shoulder. He didn't know Penny well enough to say for certain that it was or wasn't her. 'It looks like her, doesn't it?'

'Sylvie'd know for sure,' Miss Bailey said.

But when Sylvie saw it she was no more certain than Miss Bailey.

'Well, who else could it be but our Penny?' she reasoned. 'But I see what you mean, Miss Bailey. That *isn't* her smile, is it? Oh, I don't know, I feel as if everything's upside down since Penny and Mike won that competition.'

Oddly enough, another person felt that Penny had changed. In the little house in Marguerita Street, Penny had already made her presence felt, in the space of a few days. Although she was now deciding to go and take up the difficult job of the publicity campaign, she secretly wished she didn't have to. They made her so welcome, Mrs. Addy and her son Joe, and the warmth of their little circle was very comforting.

'You've only been up a day, and not a stroke of washing-up have I had to do,' Mrs. Addy said, smiling warmly at Penny. 'I'm sure I don't know what's got into you, Robina, ducks, but I will say this; you can be very taking when you like. I could wish you'd be like it all the time, but there! We are as we are made, I suppose.'

She went out and Joe came in from the garden.

'Don't mind mum, Robina,' he said softly. 'She's got a heart of gold, but you know how blunt she is.'

'If I've been thoughtless,' Penny said slowly, wondering how much she should apologise for Robina, 'I haven't meant to be, but things get very worrying at times.'

It was so hard to find the right thing to say, to make up for the way Robina had treated them, but Joe wouldn't have it.

'Don't you say things like that. You're all right, just as you are. Well, don't be so sharp with mum, of course, but treat me as you like. It doesn't matter. You're under my skin. You mean all the world to me, Robbie, no matter what you're like. You know that, don't you?'

Penny, her cheeks scorching, said at once:

'Oh, don't talk like that, Joe! You don't know what you're saying!'

'There you go again,' he marvelled. 'One minute I'm thinking how wonderful you're being to me and, as soon as I start to say what's inside me, you want to stop me! Honestly, I can't make it out, Robina.'

Penny's face flamed.

'Joe,' she said carefully, 'you know it's the stage for me always, don't you?'

Trying to say what she thought Robina would want said to him, she went on: 'I haven't had much in my life. I want nice things and fun and, the minute I see the chance, I shall take it because, if my luck changes, there is a great future in the entertainment world. Besides, well, it means everything.'

But it hurt to see Joe's face fall. Still, she had to stop him from saying those personal things to her. They were only intended for Robina's ears.

'I know I'm only a garage mechanic,' he said, earnestly, 'but I work hard. One day, when I've saved up enough, I'll have my own petrol station, and I was hoping that, well, when we were married, you'd come into the business with me.'

She shook her head and was really relieved when his mother came into the room and interrupted the conversation.

Because of Joe, Penny decided to telephone Robina and get her to come back and handle this delicate situation herself.

At that moment Robina had troubles of her own. She was sitting at her dressing-table when the telephone rang. It was Flash Farwell on the line.

'Robbie,' he said softly, as she picked up the receiver. 'Robbie, stop clowning and come back. Get me?'

She drew a deep breath and, thinking quickly, she said sharply: 'Who is that speaking? I think you must have the wrong number.'

'Oh, no, I haven't,' he said in that familiar voice that brought back the memories Robina wanted to forget, 'I'm talking to Robina Trent. I'd know that voice anywhere.'

'You're mistaken,' she said coldly. 'This is Penny Maxwell, the winner of the Curly Corn Flakes competition. I don't know how you were put through to me by the switchboard.'

'Because I asked for Penny Maxwell,' he answered, coolly. 'I've seen you up there on the stage, and I've got to hand

110

it to you — you've been carrying off a dual personality fine, but it doesn't deceive those who know you so well. Come on Robina, or Penny, or whatever you call yourself, let's stop this nonsense. Are you coming back, or shall I get the boys to fetch you? And this time you won't escape at any traffic lights.'

Robina heaved a sigh of relief.

So Flash Farwell didn't know there were two of them! He didn't know that Penny Maxwell was a different person. When he had tried to abduct Penny herself he must have thought it was Robina putting on an act, pretending not to know him!

'You've made a mistake,' she said coldly. 'My name really *is* Penny Maxwell, and I shall go to the police and report this. So you'd better stop bothering me.'

She replaced the receiver, but there was an anxious frown on her face, and when Penny herself telephoned soon afterwards to say that she was well

111

enough to take up her duties, Robina decided that it might be a good idea to arrange the switch at once.

So they met on a little wayside station, fifteen miles out of Fenmouth, where the Corn Flakes show had moved on to, that day.

There was just time to change trains. No time for Robina to do more than say she had found the job pleasant and easy. No time to warn Penny that her routine had been to get the audience singing, with light, popular, catchy tunes, instead of classical music.

As soon as she reached the hotel Walter Wiley was waiting for her.

'Now, come on, Penny lass,' he said, briskly. 'I don't know where you skipped to this afternoon, but as the show's been doing so well I'll overlook it. I don't mind telling you that you've cut the time pretty fine, though. Never mind. Give 'em all you've got, the minute you're on. Get 'em started on their own part, and warm 'em up, and I shall be happy.'

'Get them started on their own part?' Penny asked, bewildered. So far as she knew, she just had to say a few words into the microphone, and then sit down and play her beloved classical music on the white piano.

'That's right,' Walter Wiley said. 'Now get a move on, lass, though you'll have to work hard on this lot! I warn you, this town isn't going to be as easy as the last one.'

Penny hurried into the dress for the show and comforted herself in the thought that Walter Wiley would take her up to the stage and introduce her and he'd be sure to explain what he meant by the audience 'doing their part'.

The gown, a magnificent silver lame creation, overwhelmed her, and made her more apprehensive. She didn't feel right in such a dress.

'Now, lass,' Walter Wiley explained, leading her on to the stage of Fenmouth's enormous Crystal Pavilion, before the curtain rose, 'it'll be a bit different tonight. We've got special drapes, and I want you to stand here, on this little dais in the middle. The curtains rise, but the stage is in darkness. Then the spotlight comes down on you, and you hold it for a minute. Then you take over and it's all yours.'

He left her with a confident smile and a nod, but Penny panicked. This wasn't what she had expected at all, and he had gone before she could ask for more details. Surely he didn't expect her to take over where Robina left off, without a little help?

And then, with a swish, the curtains rose and a sea of blurry faces in the gloom below told Penny that this was indeed the moment. The spotlight came on, blinding her, and the expectant hush of the audience seemed to last for ever.

Walter Wiley, watching from the wings with one or two other people connected with the publicity campaign, felt that thrill which Robina instilled into him every time she went on alone and handled a new audience. He waited to see what she would do tonight.

Then the smile abruptly left his face. Something was wrong.

Instead of slowly turning her head and flinging her arms wide, the girl on the stage started to move hesitantly and then, with distress all over her face, she half turned towards the wings, mutely imploring him to help her.

Transfixed, helpless, Penny stood there, in the grip of stage fright.

Walter Wiley strode forward on to the stage. What was the matter with Penny? Was she ill?

He was used to taking charge of awkward situations. With a bright smile, he turned to the audience, at the same time taking Penny's hand, and gently urging her to the centre of the stage.

'Ladies and gentlemen,' he began confidently, 'as you know, our advance billing warned you of a surprise. And lovely Penny Maxwell, who was the winner of our great competition is certainly a surprise packet! She's taken audiences by storm on our triumphant tour, and tonight she's going to give you something different. Now, give her a big hand!'

The audience dutifully applauded, but it wasn't the spontaneous delighted roar of welcome which Robina usually commanded. They were clapping because he had suggested that they should. In Walter Wiley they recognised the polished showman. Whatever had threatened to go wrong he now had it in hand. They waited, to see what would happen next.

Walter took Penny over to the big white piano, smiling encouragingly.

'What's wrong?' he whispered. 'Not ill, are you?'

As Penny shook her head, he said briskly:

'Well, get going then, and give 'em all you've got!'

Penny felt better once she was at the piano. But she hadn't bargained on being pushed out there alone to face an audience for the first time in her life. She had expected Walter Wiley to go with her, and do the talking. So she determinedly forgot about the audience and started to play.

She was good. Walter Wiley, anxiously watching from the wings, had to admit that. But she played classical music and, though she was obviously enjoying herself now, she wasn't pulling the audience in to share her enjoyment. She seemed to have forgotten them.

He was glad when it was over. Penny had recovered sufficiently to bow nicely to the audience and Walter Wiley went on to escort her off the stage. But from his point of view that performance had been a flop.

'Now then let's have it!' he began, once they were alone in her dressing-room. 'What was wrong with you?'

Penny was surprised.

'I'm sorry, Mr. Wiley, but considering it was my first appearance, is it surprising?'

'First appearance?' he echoed blankly.

'What are you talking about?'

'You seem disappointed in me, but I don't think I've ever played better although I started off so badly. I don't know what Robina's been doing — '

'*Robina?*' He shouted dumbfounded.

'Mr. Wiley,' she said, earnestly, 'I'm sorry I let you down but, honestly, I was too ill to have gone on to the stage for the first few shows. I thought it was the next best thing to get someone else to take my place and, as she looked so much like me, it almost seemed like Providence.'

Walter Wiley's face began to clear.

'D'you mean to say there are two of you?'

Penny nodded.

He began to think quickly. It all fitted in. He had caught himself thinking on several occasions that this wasn't Penny Maxwell at all, but a complete stranger. And then he had dismissed the thought as absurd.

'Well, why didn't you say so at first?'

'I didn't know it until I was ill, and

she came to my hotel bedroom,' Penny explained quickly, and briefly told him what she remembered of that painful interview, when she had felt so ill. 'She promised she'd explain everything to you and, if you agreed, she'd be willing to step into my shoes until I was well again.'

'Well, she said nothing to me about it!' he exploded. 'I thought it was you, doing fine! We all did. We thought you were a bit shy at first, till you got used to the idea. Now, what are we going to do?'

'I don't understand,' Penny frowned.

'Well, it's obvious after the way she took hold of audiences that we can't have you going on and standing there like that! Oh, I'm sorry for you, lass, I've got a good idea what stage fright is like. Seen it before. But, after all, you said you were going to be a concert pianist, didn't you?'

'Well, that's different,' Penny retorted. 'When I become a concert pianist I shall just walk out to the piano and play. Someone else will announce me.'

'Yes, I know,' he agreed, at once contrite. 'I'm sorry, lass. I didn't mean to go for you. Wasn't your fault. It's just such a howling disappointment, to find someone who could do the job just as we wanted it.'

'I know!' Penny sympathised. 'But the remedy's in your hands.'

'Eh?' he asked startled.

'*I* don't want to do it, and Robina *does*! She loves that sort of thing. She's an actress and she's out of a job at the moment. Why don't you let her continue in my place?'

Walter Wiley hesitated.

'Well, I don't know. I suppose we *could* do that, but we couldn't let you give up the thing altogether. It was your photo and you were the prize-winner. You'd have to be seen sometimes.'

'Then let me send for Robina. I know where she lives,' Penny urged.

'You mean to say you don't want to be the most envied girl on the South

Coast? You wouldn't mind?' he asked.

'All I want is to be free to go ahead with my music,' Penny replied simply.

'Well, I can't make any arrangements myself,' Walter Wiley said slowly, 'but I'll see my directors and let you know what they've got to say about it.'

He took Penny out to her car. It was late, and she refused his kind offer to take her out to dinner. She just wanted to go to bed and rest.

It was a short drive along the front to her hotel.

Penny sighed and saw with dismay the well-dressed crowds churning round the entrance of the biggest hotel in the place.

She got out of the car but, as she walked across the pavement, under the striped awning leading to the hotel steps, someone in the crowd plucked at her skirt. People were saying things about her, recognising her, and she thought it was another fan who touched her, until she heard a man's voice say: '*Robina*!'

121

She froze in her tracks but she couldn't stop herself from looking round to see who had spoken.

As the crowds churned around her she saw his face. Her feet were galvanised into action and she almost pushed a way through the crush as she fled up the steps and into the lift. It was the face of the man who had tried to kidnap her that day in London.

8

Penny was shaking when she reached her room. She shut and locked the door feverishly.

Then reason reasserted itself. It wasn't Penny Maxwell they wanted. Hadn't he said 'Robina'? It was that other girl. But Penny's heart wouldn't ease up in its mad tattoo. Every sound woke her through that long night and she decided to telephone Walter Wiley first thing in the morning.

Walter Wiley, however, put that resolution out of her mind by calling her first.

'Penny, lass, you can stop worrying. Get your pal Robina, pronto, will you? If she can't come at once, I promise you I'll give you only light jobs to do. You know the sort of thing — being led on to the stage and smiling nicely and playing a bit of music here and there.'

'Oh, thank you, Mr. Wiley!' Penny gasped, and it wasn't until she rang off that she realised that her relief over his decision had put out of her mind her resolve to tell him about the men who had tried to kidnap her and about the man in the crowd last night.

Penny telephoned to the little house in Marguerita Street, from Fenmouth Station. She didn't want to use the hotel telephones in case their secret leaked out.

Robina didn't sound too pleased when she heard Penny's voice.

'What's wrong?' she asked. 'Isn't it working out?'

'Robina, I thought you'd be pleased to hear my news. Walter Wiley wants you back,' Penny said.

Instead of the excited outburst that she had expected Penny found that Robina was rather cautious.

'Well, don't you want to go on with what you started?' Penny asked, in surprise. 'I thought you rather enjoyed taking my place.'

'That was *then*,' Robina said.

'Well, what's happened since? Have you got other engagements? I don't want to put you out, Robina.'

'I mean, we'd have to have some sort of settlement,' Robina explained, 'if I came again. Last time it was only for a few days. This might go on for some time. I should want paying for it. After all, it might lose me some other booking!'

'Oh, Robina,' Penny said in exasperation, 'they'll see you're all right. After all, it's your talent they want and I haven't got any to offer them.'

'It's not only that,' Robina said, and she didn't sound very friendly. 'It's the situation here. I don't know what you said or did, but things are very awkward.'

'You mean, Mrs. Addy's son Joe?' Penny asked quickly.

'You've guessed right,' Robina said tartly. 'I don't know what you could have done to mess it all up in so short a time but if I'm going to get you out of a hole again, I suggest you do the same for me.'

Robina was speaking guardedly. Penny recalled that the telephone at No. 7 was in the small hall. She said, to show that she understood what Robina meant; 'You mean you want me to take your place, in your digs, and pretend to be you again?'

Robina ignored the reluctance in Penny's voice and said firmly: 'That's just what I do mean and, unless you agree to that, there's nothing doing.'

★ ★ ★

When Penny went back to Walter Wiley she was surprised to find how eager he was to hear about Robina.

'She can't come until tomorrow,' Penny said, 'but she will be giving up the chance of some good bookings, so she wants — '

'Oh, that's all right. I'll make it worth her while,' Walter Wiley said easily. 'Now let's think this thing out. We go to

Sherwood Bay this afternoon. You must appear yourself, as it's so near to your home town, and someone would be sure to spot a stranger in your place. We'll just have you up there on the stage looking pretty. Nice and easy.'

'Thank you,' Penny whispered. She was curiously shy about appearing so near home.

Walter Wiley watched her thoughtfully.

'You'll have to do an evening show as well, then we can move on to Seelands-sands the next day, when your pal comes. But you can have a few hours off to pop over to Elmdale. I expect you'll want to look up old friends.'

'Yes, I should like that,' Penny said gratefully.

The chauffeur driven car which the company had put at her disposal whirled Penny over to Elmdale that afternoon, but she asked the man to stop at the market cross, and wait for her behind the old inn known as The

Whippet. She went quietly on foot to the little row of shops where she had once worked, and dreamed of music, and of Paul Hambledon.

It was early closing day. Penny, who had lost all sense of time in the anxieties of the past week, had forgotten it, and her disappointment was sharp. Mrs. Drew was out, so she went along to Miss Bailey's and found her in, finishing off a dress for someone.

'Penny!' she exclaimed, and Penny rushed to give her a big hug. 'But I never expected to see you, of all people!'

'We were in Sherwood Bay this afternoon. Will you come and see me tonight? I'm sorry it's short notice. So much has been happening.'

She broke off, biting her lip. She couldn't tell Miss Bailey what was happening without disclosing about that other girl. Walter Wiley was insistent that the secret should be kept.

'Yes, I know,' Miss Bailey said, her smile fading. 'Mike and Sylvie were a bit hurt, I don't mind telling you. Pity they're both out or you could have seen them and answered a question for them that's been bothering them a bit.'

'What question?' Penny asked startled.

'Well, it was the way you spoke to them when they phoned you to say good-bye.'

'But I didn't . . . ' Penny began, and then bit her lip. 'I mean, I didn't want them to be hurt, but it's all been such a mad rush. You understand, don't you?'

Miss Bailey's face changed.

'Yes, I understand,' she said, but she didn't sound as if she understood one bit. Penny was thinking fast. Robina didn't say she had spoken to them, but that must be the explanation. She wondered what Robina could have said to them to make Miss Bailey look at her like that.

'I hate this new life,' Penny said suddenly.

Miss Bailey looked surprised.

'Well, now, from all accounts, Penny, I should have thought you'd taken to it like a duck takes to water.'

'Don't be misled by appearances,' Penny said impulsively, going up to Miss Bailey and taking her hands. 'Believe me, my friends are here, in Elmdale, and if I thought anything had changed I'd be very unhappy.'

'I wish I could believe you mean that,' Miss Bailey said slowly. Then with an effort at hospitality she added: 'I expect you'd like a cup of tea. I was just making one.'

'No, please don't trouble,' Penny said, feeling a little awkward with her old friend. 'Mrs. Drew's out. Is she all right?'

'It's all just about the same as when you went away,' Miss Bailey said quietly, looking at Penny.

'Have you heard how Paul Hambledon's getting on?' Penny forced herself to ask.

'Seems he's doing fine for himself. Got a job in Wesley's in Sherwood Bay, running the music department. At least, it appears he's playing the piano there.

Why don't you go over and see for yourself?'

'Yes, perhaps I will,' Penny said, grateful for the excuse to get away. It was no longer the same.

There was a lump in her throat as she left Miss Bailey's shop. Is that what happened to girls who won competitions and sprang into the limelight overnight? Didn't their old friends feel they could be on the same easy footing any more? Or had Robina said something so dreadful to Mike and Sylvie that they had all been so hurt that friendship was no longer possible?

Penny went back to the car and asked the chauffeur to drive her over to Sherwood Bay.

The bay looked brighter and more prosperous than Penny could have believed to be possible.

Then she was outside Wesley's. She walked along the length of the windows and, quite suddenly, she was staring in at the music window, where Paul Hambledon sat playing.

She felt an odd sensation as she looked at him, just as if a knife were turning in her heart. He hadn't bothered to look her up while she was in London. He hadn't made any attempt to get into touch with her and, although he must have seen her name on the posters in Sherwood Bay, she had had no word from him. Yet he was here, all the time, playing the piano in this store!

Suddenly she was aware of Paul staring at her.

He was so astonished to see her there that he stopped playing for a moment. Then, remembering where he was, he smiled at the crowd and, finishing the number, he got up and went into the interior of the shop.

Penny eased her way out of the crowd. It seemed to her that he hadn't even wanted to speak to her, now that he had seen her looking in the window! She swallowed hard on the lump in her throat, and told herself that she had been a fool to expect anything else.

As she hurried past the door she almost cannoned into Paul as he came out, looking for her. They both stood still, staring at each other.

'Paul! I came to see — that is, Miss Bailey said you were working near Elmdale. I'm so glad you've got a job,' Penny stammered, flushing.

He stared at Penny as if he couldn't take his eyes off her. This was the girl he remembered, with her sweet, earnest little face, and her eager, friendly voice.

'*You came to see me?*' he echoed, in wonderment. 'Why, Penny, what's happened? You're so different from the last time I saw you!'

Penny's smile faded a little and Paul put the wrong construction on it.

'Perhaps I shouldn't have said that,' he put in quickly, before she could attempt to speak. 'I know it must be rather tiresome to have friends calling, when you're in the middle of fittings and important luncheons and everything.'

'Honestly, I don't know what you're

talking about,' Penny said, and almost succumbed to the temptation of telling him in confidence about the arrangement with Robina.

But Paul gave her no chance to say anything.

'I think you do,' he said quietly. 'Never mind, it's very nice to see you here, anyway, and I'm happy to think you could find time in your busy life to come and see me.'

And he meant it. He felt very badly, at times like this, about losing his money, and having to hold down a difficult and at times irksome job. It was a blow that he should have no money, now that there was someone like Penny to spend it on.

But Penny didn't realise that he felt like that. She still thought of him as a member of an old country family. She looked on herself still as just a girl who was employed in a baker's shop and, to hear Paul Hambledon talk like that, suggested to her that he was making fun of her. He was the second person to hurt her that day.

'I only meant to come and see how you were getting on,' she said swiftly. 'I wasn't meaning to come and bother you. I know you must be busy.'

The manager, who liked to come along to see the effect of Paul's playing on the crowds outside, happened to be passing just then.

He looked across at Penny and frowned.

'I'd better hurry. I have another show, anyway,' she said, and she turned and walked quickly away, melting into the crowds before Paul had a chance to speak.

The manager went over to him.

'Isn't that the girl the Corn Flakes people are boosting, Hambledon? The winner of the competition?'

Paul looked rather bewildered.

'Yes, sir. I was just going to bring her over to you, but she went before I had a chance to say anything.'

'How well do you know her? We ought to be able to do something about this, if she's a friend of yours.'

They walked back into the store. Penny paused, and wondered if Paul would get into trouble. It might be as well, perhaps, to go back and explain to Paul's chief that it wasn't his fault.

She went back again, but entered the store by a door further down. She had a good view of the music department. Paul was standing beside his piano, talking to someone. It was Audrey Bayfield. Penny hesitated, wondering how long it would be before Paul was free. As she waited by the records counter she heard one assistant say to another, with a nod towards Audrey Bayfield: 'She likes folk to know she's the boss, now she's inherited Wesley's from her great-uncle. It looks as though she's hooked Paul Hambledon, too. Some girls have all the luck.'

* * *

Penny made her two short appearances that day and didn't get stage fright. It

136

was much easier because Walter Wiley helped her over the difficult bits.

The following day, Robina, looking smart and casual and not in the least bothered, took over, and saw to it that she was seen about in the luxurious car belonging to the company, and she lunched with Walter Wiley in the best hotel.

Penny went back to London with a sense of relief. Now, at last, she could arrange for her music lessons.

The music school was very important-looking, but the people were kind, and the sound of music coming from different rooms gave Penny a thrill of delight.

It was just as she left the school that she noticed the car drawn up at the kerb. Before she could hurry away, a familiar figure got out and held the door open.

'Get in, Robbie, or do I have to make you?' that dreaded voice asked.

He took Penny's arm, as she stood frozen to the spot, and propelled her into the car. It was all done so quickly that, again, she had been caught napping, and was too late to offer resistance.

He sat back in the car with her. Another man was driving. Penny stole a look at her companion and decided that she must at last get to the bottom of this. His swarthy, long face, with its thin dark moustache and sideboards, was grim but not unkindly. Obviously a foreigner, he had little trace of accent, and merely looked irritated at the difficulty he was having to get her back.

'Look, I'm Penny Maxwell, not Robina Trent,' Penny said desperately. 'Won't you believe that?'

He smiled.

'You make me tired. Drop it, Robbie, and let's get down to business. And I'm going to keep hold of your arm this time. Now listen — and don't tell me you're going to the police. You and I know why. *You couldn't*. If you just opened your mouth once about me, I'd soon let them know what you've been up to, since we first — er — met.'

Penny's eyes widened. Was Robina Trent a criminal, then? But Penny couldn't believe that. The man must know something about her but it didn't necessarily mean that she was wanted by the police.

Penny slumped against the seat, feeling trapped and helpless, and the man beside her took it to mean that she was giving in to him.

'That's better. Now, it's a very simple thing I want you to do this time. Remember my new club, The Red Shoe?'

She nodded, because he seemed to expect that.

'I want someone to play the piano. Oh, and something else, of course! I want you to wear a certain nice necklace for me and, when a man comes by, I'll point out to you the one I mean, all you have to do is to unfasten the clasp and let it drop off as you're taking your bow. He will pick it up. You don't have to notice that you've dropped it. Act surprised when he gives it back. Get me?'

'What would I do that for?' Penny gasped.

'That's my girl! Pretend to be innocent and you'll carry the thing off with flying colours. Now then, tonight at eight. You know the address. 2A, St. Agnes's Court.'

He let go of her arm and told the driver to stop.

'Oh, and wear something very nice,' he ordered.

To Penny's relief and surprise, the car stopped and he opened the door for her. She was free.

9

Marguerita Street looked smaller than when Penny saw it last. If it hadn't been for the presence of Joe Addy she might have been glad to go back. Joe's mother was a dear.

Joe was a problem, Penny reflected. She hoped he wouldn't be in, but he was. He had seen her coming up the steps and opened the door for her.

'Robina, I had to see you the minute you came in! You know I hate having words with you, but it wasn't entirely my fault, you must admit!'

Penny's heart sank. So Robina had been quarrelling with him!

'Oh, forget it, Joe,' Penny said, and went to go past him up to Robina's little room.

Joe took her arm, his face lighting up.

'Come to the pictures with me tonight, just to prove that you meant it.'

'I'm sorry, Joe, but I can't,' she said. 'Not tonight. I'm booked up. A job.'

'Oh, good! I'm so glad. Where is it Robbie?'

'Tell you later, Joe,' she said. 'No time now,' and she ran upstairs. She couldn't tell him anything about it until she found out if Robina had let him know her secret.

Robina. Angrily, Penny decided that she would have to telephone Robina about it.

She tried to recall, as she hurried out again, and down to the public call-box in the next street, what Robina had said that first time they had met in Penny's hotel bedroom, when she had told Robina about the kidnapping. Robina had merely expressed sympathy for an awful experience which Penny had had. And yet, she must have known at once that they were her old associates, thinking they had found Robina herself!

Luck with with Penny. She caught Robina in her hotel.

'I must speak to you, Robina! Those

people who tried to kidnap me — they caught me again today. Who are they?'

Robina was angry. 'For goodness' sake have a bit of sense and don't call me up like this, unless you want to mess everything up!'

'But you've got to tell me. The only way I could get away from them was to promise to do as they wanted. Play the piano in a club the man was running.'

There was a pause and then Robina's voice, its anger gone, came through clearly.

'Oh, *him*! That's Flash Farwell. He's all right.'

'He didn't seem 'all right' to me,' Penny retorted.

'You had me worried for a minute,' Robina said, almost gaily now, as she thought quickly at the other end of the line. 'Why don't you go? He'll pay you, and it'll be something towards that musical career of yours. Experience, too. I should! You do as he says and he'll be all right with you.'

She rang off before Penny could say another word.

Penny looked doubtfully at the telephone, but Robina had really sounded as if she meant it, when she said that Flash Farwell was all right.

Perhaps all her fears were for nothing, Penny told herself. Anyway, it was only to play the piano and drop a necklace, which must be part of the act. There couldn't be any harm in that.

Penny found a red evening gown among Robina's things, and a short fur jacket to put over it. When she was ready she slipped out and called a taxi.

St. Agnes's Court was in a shabby little alley behind the bright lights of the West End. Down some narrow stone steps she went, until she came to a door with a grill.

A man's face appeared and asked her what she wanted.

'Flash Farwell said . . . ' Penny began, when, to her surprise, the door opened quickly.

'Sorry, Robbie, didn't recognise you

at first! Where have you been all this time?' he said, a huge smile broadening over his face. 'Better let me show you the way, you don't know this place, do you?' and he took her through to where Flash was, in a tiny office.

Several people who worked for Flash Farwell greeted her that evening, thinking she was Robina. Flash fastened the necklace he had spoken of round her neck and showed her how to operate the spring clasp at a touch. It was a heavy necklace of large stones surrounded by small ones, each hinged to the next.

The piano was painted blue, with gold and silver stars all over it.

'Play what you like,' Flash said, 'but don't show off. Keep it soft. They don't want to listen to the music. They just want a background to their conversation. Get me, Robbie?'

Penny nodded in bewilderment, but did as he asked. The people in the softly lit room with its little tables and chairs, talked and laughed, drank and ate, and took no notice of her. The necklace incident went off without a hitch and Penny, vastly relieved, was free to go.

Flash put some notes into her hand and said casually: 'Same time next week, Robbie — and don't let me have to fetch you. Okay?'

Penny nodded and escaped.

Somehow she got through the next day or two without any difficult patches with Joe Addy. She found out the time he was at home from the garage and took care to be out then. She ate out, and started her music practice in a studio where a piano could be rented.

Then, just as she was settling down, she was called back to Sherwood Bay by Walter Wiley, for a personal appearance.

'It's a function, my lass, that you'll have to undertake because so many of your local people will be there,' he explained when Penny arrived. 'They want to give you a private and personal 'do' to show how glad they are at your success. Posh dinner and dance, and nothing to scare you. You just have to smile and say thank you.'

Penny was deeply touched and, when she arrived, she was given a very warm welcome.

As she sat at a table with some old friends Paul Hambledon appeared from out of the crowd.

He walked straight over to her table and said: 'May I have the pleasure of this dance, Penny?'

It was the first time she had seen him in evening dress, and her heart lifted with pride. He looked so tall and distinguished.

As she stood up, with a little smile, she was conscious of the quickening of her heartbeats and, as he whirled her into the centre of the floor, there was the click of cameras and the flash of bulbs.

They danced in companionable silence for a while.

'You look very lovely, Penny,' he said at last, his lips against her ear. 'Why did you run away the other day? I wanted you to meet the chief.'

'I didn't want you to get into trouble for wasting the firm's time,' Penny explained. 'Besides, I heard that you are now working for Miss Bayfield.'

'It's the merest coincidence that Miss Bayfield inherited the business that happened to be employing me,' he said, stiffly.

'Did I say the wrong thing?' Penny faltered.

His face broke into a tender little smile.

'No. No, little Penny. It was I who did that. Forgive me. I'm still touchy about having to work for someone else. Let me show you how sorry I am. It's my half-day tomorrow. Spend it with me. Say you will!'

'Well, I don't get much time — ' Penny murmured, remembering just in time that she had to go back to London, leaving Robina to carry on. 'But I'd love to if I could. May I find out if I can get away, and send a note to let you know?'

'Yes. Send it to me at Wesley's, will you?' he said, and seemed genuinely pleased.

Almost before Penny realised what was happening, Audrey Bayfield came up to them and possessively took Paul's arm.

'I wondered what was happening to you,' she said, smiling up at him and ignoring Penny. 'I thought that was our dance, but it seems I was mistaken.'

'The next is our dance, Audrey,' Paul said, and he bowed to Penny and led Audrey away.

'She *is* a cat,' a girl murmured audibly behind Penny, but added ruefully: 'She's got him well in tow, though.'

Penny's cheeks scorched. She wished she hadn't heard that, but she couldn't very well get out of earshot in time.

She found that her eyes were searching all the time for Paul. She kept getting glimpses of his dark head very close to the ash-blonde one; a flash of that lovely lilac velvet gown which

Audrey wore, and her fabulous necklace and ear-rings.

Penny suddenly felt that she could bear it no longer. She went to the cloak-room, believing Audrey was still dancing with Paul. It would be nice to get away somewhere by herself, and repair her make-up and cool her aching head.

She was surprised to find, however, that Audrey was there. She looked at Penny with a patronising smile.

'Enjoying yourself?' she drawled.

'Very much, thank you,' Penny said, with a little lift of the chin.

'I'm glad. I wouldn't like Paul Hambledon to spoil things for you.'

'What do you mean?' Penny asked.

'Oh, well, you know how it is. He's in the limelight now and he's always been rich and spoiled. Of course, I can't see any wrong in my Paul but I can't help feeling sorry for the girls he keeps asking to go out with him, knowing there's nothing in it for them. He didn't ask you to go out with him, I hope?'

'It's kind of you to worry about me,' Penny replied, with dignity, 'but I assure you I can take care of myself.'

She finished powdering her nose and, gathering up her things, she went out of the room.

She was shaking with anger and indignation, but however she viewed the situation, however much she reminded herself of how pleased Paul seemed to be to see her — she couldn't get out of her head the bit of conversation she had overheard, and Audrey's 'my Paul' kept ringing in her ears.

When she was back in her own room again she thrashed out the problem until long after midnight. Finally, she decided that she must write Paul a letter.

'*Dear Paul,*' she wrote, after much careful thought, '*I am not coming out with you, much as I would have liked to. I realise now that you are just being kind to me, as Miss Bayfield quite rightly pointed out this evening, when she explained the situation to me. So this must be goodbye, but I do wish you all the very best for your future happiness with her. Penny.'*

She did as he asked her and addressed it to him at Wesley's emporium, but it never reached him. Audrey, who was waiting for Paul to come down from the manager's room, where there had been a discussion about the song competition, said she would give it to him.

Audrey guessed who it was from, the minute she saw the name of the hotel on the back of the envelope. After the slightest hesitation, she strolled into a quiet corner and ripped it open. What she read made her cheeks flame with anger and, without a second thought, she tore it into small pieces and dropped it into a nearby waste bin.

* * *

Penny decided when she reached London that she would think of nothing else but her music lessons. It shouldn't be too difficult. She believed that Flash Farwell would stop bothering her now that she had promised to play for him at his club once a week.

But if Penny thought her problems were over, she had reckoned without Joe Addy. Delightedly he met her on the stairs.

'Gosh, I've got great news, Robina! Remember I said I couldn't get a holiday this year on account of it being a new job? Well, the boss is so pleased with the way I've been slaving for him that he's given me a week after all. A week with pay!'

'How nice for you, Joe,' Penny said sincerely.

'No, not how nice for *me* Robina,' he said earnestly. 'Nice for both of us. Remember what you promised?'

Penny stared blankly at Joe.

She had no idea what to say, without giving away the whole wretched business.

Joe misunderstood her silence. His smile faded.

'I suppose you're sorry you suggested it,' he said, and the look on his good-natured face hurt her.

'No, no, I'm not, Joe! It's just that — well, how could it be managed?' she finished lamely.

Joe didn't notice that she didn't know what he was talking about.

'Well, easily, as I see it!' he said, his enthusiasm returning. 'This job of yours — it was only for one night, wasn't it?'

'One night each week,' Penny admitted slowly. She dare not let him know about her music lessons.

'Well, there you are then!' he said excitedly. 'Between now and the next time you have to go to your job we could work in our week's holiday. Robina, you did really *want* to go to the sea with me when you made that promise, didn't you? You weren't just leading me on?'

Penny felt a little relieved. It wasn't so bad as she had anticipated.

'Well, Joe, I hadn't any work at the

time, and it *will* be a bit difficult just now. Can't you go away yourself and, if I can get away, I'll join you for a day or two?'

'Well, all right,' he reluctantly agreed. 'I might have known you wouldn't keep your promise and I can't help feeling that you'll wriggle out of even two days away with me. Why do I have to be such a fool over you, Robina?'

Penny was deeply touched. Joe was too nice a fellow to be treated like this. In her heart, she didn't really think that Robina would keep her promise about his holiday, even if she could get away.

'I will *try*,' Penny promised, 'if it's only for *one* day, and if I can manage more I'll let you know.'

'Where'd you want it to be?' he persisted.

Feeling that she was getting deeper and deeper into the tangle with every passing moment, Penny said wildly:

'Well, what about Redsands?'

It was the first place that came into her head. She thought Joe might like it, as it was a big, popular place, and also the Corn Flakes campaign had already been there, so it would be safe.

Joe looked a trifle disappointed, but he seemed to expect Robina to make such a choice.

'Anywhere to make you happy, Robina,' he said. 'I'll fix it all up.'

When he had left Penny she felt the panic rising in her. Then commonsense asserted itself. Joe wouldn't be able to fix up anything in such a hurry. It was well on into the season. Everywhere would be booked long ago. The spell of hot weather was crowding out the big resorts. No, it looked as if both she and Robina were safe from this new problem.

Penny telephoned Robina as soon as she could. She felt she must tell her about this new development with Joe Addy.

Robina sounded angry.

'Don't keep calling me up about things like that!' she said furiously. 'It simply isn't important. Oh, yes, I know

Joe Addy's been on about this holiday of his for ages. I said I'd think about it. It wasn't a promise and I had to do something to keep him quiet. It's bad luck that he should have managed to get a holiday after all, but you'll just have to cope with things as you think best.'

Without giving Penny time to reply, Robina rang off.

Penny felt helpless as she stood there looking at the receiver. It just wasn't any use appealing to Robina. She had no heart.

She went back to Mrs. Addy's house, and tidied herself before going down to join them for her evening meal.

Mrs. Addy dished up an appetising meal, and smiled across at Penny.

'What have you been up to today, Robina? Any luck with those agents? I will say this for you, you're a sticker! Out every morning, plugging at it all day to find work. I wish you could get something good.'

'She *has* got a job, once a week,

mum,' Joe put in, coming in at the back door at that moment, and starting to wash his hands at the sink. 'But we don't want her fixed up for the next week. She's going to take that holiday with me.'

Penny shot him a startled glance.

'Only if it can be managed, Joe,' she reminded him.

'Well, it can!' he shouted, plunging his head under the tap, and towelling his face vigorously until it shone. 'A chap I know has got an aunt who lives in Redsands. Only a small house, mind you, but she can let us have a couple of rooms, and she'll take care of our food all right. Now, Robina, what do you say?'

Penny averted her eyes. It was useless. She just couldn't say anything that would take away the shining happiness from his face.

And then Robina's words came back to her. 'Cope with things as best you can.'

'I don't think I can manage a full

week, Joe,' she said, in a stifled voice, 'but if I can be back in time for my job, that one night next week, then — '

'Robbie!' Joe cried, delightedly, coming round the table to her with outstretched hands. 'D'you really mean it?'

Penny thought for one wild moment that he was going to take her into his arms and kiss her. But Mrs. Addy saved the situation.

'All right, all right, Joe! She's said she'll go with you, so now let's all sit down to supper. You can both talk it over afterwards.'

Mrs. Addy and Joe ate a hearty meal but, for Penny, the food threatened to choke her. What had she done? It was all very well trying to do something to save Joe being hurt, but suppose she couldn't keep him at a friendly distance until Robina came back to relieve her from this awful situation?

10

Robina was getting used to being the pampered pet of the Corn Flakes campaign. With no anxiety about what she would do for money tomorrow or the next day, she found that her work was easy. She was a success.

She wasn't satisfied, however. She wanted security for the future. The rich men who took her about, offered nothing permanent. What lay ahead of her when the campaign ended?

She put it to Walter Wiley as they dined one night after the day's activities.

'Will I get anything else, after the season's over, here on the coast, Walter?'

He stopped smiling across the flower-decked table at her and thoughtfully sipped his wine.

'Oh, well, now, lass, let's wait and

see, shall we? Aren't we paying you enough for being stop-gap to Penny Maxwell?'

'Stop-gap! What a hateful word! Aren't I any good on my own?' she stormed.

'Well, you're having a good time, aren't you, till your own stage work comes along again?'

'D'you think I want to go back to all that? Cheap lodgings and cheap food, travelling all night on draughty trains, and never knowing for sure what the next engagement will bring? Why can't I have a contract with you people, for the publicity?'

'Look, I thought we'd gone all over that before,' he said wearily. 'Don't let's spoil a pleasant evening.'

'D'you mean to say you meant it when you said Penny Maxwell was to be the one to get the sittings and the model work and all the other things that didn't entail going on the stage and handling an audience? It isn't fair! It's a shame!'

'But you did agree to it,' he pointed out mildly.

'It isn't in writing,' she said swiftly.

He sighed.

'Let's dance. You're tired, that's what it is. We can't have a lovely girl like you, looking all sullen and fed-up with life generally. Come on, Robbie.'

He, too, had started to use her pet name, but with a difference. There was a warmth about the way he held her as they danced. She knew he liked her. As she danced, Robina thought quickly. The other men who were attracted to her had made it plain that they weren't thinking of marriage. They just wanted to take out and about the success girl of the seaside season. Robina wanted more than that.

Well, what was wrong with Walter Wiley? He was young and attractive and had an awfully good job with the Corn Flakes concern. One day he'd probably be a director.

'You make me dance on air,' she murmured, deciding to play up to him.

'You're a fine dancer, that's why,' he said.

His thoughts strayed to that night when the Sherwood Bay people gave the dance and dinner for Penny Maxwell, and he remembered Penny in her foaming white dress. 'Penny Maxwell dances beautifully, too,' he said.

Robina stiffened in his arms, but he didn't appear to notice that she didn't answer him. He went on thoughtfully.

'You know, I'll never get over the likeness between you two girls. It's uncanny. You might be twins. You sure you never had a sister?'

'Quite sure,' Robina said, rather shortly. She wasn't interested enough in Penny to want to talk about her while she was dancing with Walter Wiley. 'Most women dance well,' she said, bringing the conversation back to the dancing. 'But it's a different thing with men. You dance better than most men, and you don't seem to be aware of it. You do most things well, Walter.'

She looked up into his face, to see

how he was taking that bit of praise.

'Oh, go on,' he laughed. 'I'm just average.'

'That's just what you're not,' she told him. 'You're quite the reverse, in fact. Look at you, the things you do so well. And look how sweet you are to me, too, lending me a bit whenever I run short, and never saying a word about it. You never seem to realise how nice you are. A bit of a dark horse, too. No one seems to know a thing about you!'

He stopped smiling, and looked guarded.

'Oh, who wants to know anything about me?' he said, trying to laugh the subject off. But Robina wouldn't have it.

'Tell me about yourself. Where do you live?'

'Oh, I'm all over the place. Wherever the company sends me, like this season, for instance.'

'And when you're not — all over the place?'

'Look, do we have to talk about me, Robina?'

She was quick to notice his tone and stopped at once. There would be plenty of time to find out more about him. What worried her much more was what would happen to her if Penny was going to get all the good things and she, Robina, had to go back to Marguerita Street. For that reason she must keep in with Penny.

It was then that Walter Wiley's words came back to her and gave her an idea. The sister angle had been worked before by other people. Suppose she could convince Penny that she was her sister? They might even share a flat together, with all that money Penny had won, and all she would be likely to make in the future from advertising the Corn Flakes.

Also, there was the business of Flash Farwell. If Penny could be made to think that Robina was her sister, she might also be persuaded to take Robina's place indefinitely with Flash and his friends. Until —

Until Robina could bring Walter Wiley to think in terms of marriage.

★　★　★

Paul Hambledon waited for the note which Penny had promised him, and when it didn't come he began to wonder if anything had happened to her. He knew where she had been staying but, when he telephoned, he was told that the Corn Flake people had moved on to their next town.

'Paul,' Audrey said, as she faced him at lunch the next day, 'whatever is the matter with you? I've spoken to you twice but you haven't even heard me.'

'Sorry. I was wondering if anything had happened to Penny Maxwell. She said she'd let me hear from her about a trip I suggested.'

Audrey bit her lip.

'Perhaps she thought better of it, Paul. You know, it's common knowledge any number of men are taking her around. Everyone's calling her a good-time girl.'

'I don't believe that,' he said quietly, 'and, if they are, then they're wrong. She has to be seen about with people. It's all part of the publicity.'

Audrey shrugged and said lightly.

'Oh, well, then, stop worrying. What about this song competition of yours? You're not losing interest, are you?'

'No. No, of course not. But the public are, I think. What we need is — well the original girl, I suppose?'

Audrey whitened.

'Do you mean to tell me you composed that music for Penny Maxwell?'

'Well, of course,' Paul smiled.

'Wonderful inspiration for you, she must have been,' commented Audrey, with sweet sarcasm, which was quite lost on Paul.

'And if we can only get the Corn Flakes company to let us have her for half an hour one afternoon,' Paul went on, 'it would be jolly good publicity for us as well as the Corn Flakes people.'

'Good heavens!' Audrey exclaimed. 'They'll probably want an enormous fee for the loan of their pampered pet.'

'You don't know,' Paul objected quietly. 'They might be willing to get a bit more publicity for themselves.'

Audrey bit her lip and looked down. She was beaten and she knew it. She didn't want to pay a fee for Penny's services and yet she was only too well aware that she couldn't afford to lose the publicity which would result from Penny's appearance at Wesley's, if it could be arranged.

'Very well,' Audrey replied stiffly. 'I'll think it over.'

* * *

Mike and Sylvie were in Redsands that afternoon for their half-day off. Redsands was Sylvie's choice, and Mike was puzzled.

'I'd have thought you'd want to go to Willowbeach, seeing that the Corn

Flakes show is there,' he said.

'That's just why I didn't want to go to Willowbeach,' Sylvie explained miserably, 'although I like Willowbeach better than Redsands. I just couldn't bear to see Penny again.'

Mike leaned beside her at the rails and watched the children below in the paddling pool.

'I think you're wrong about Penny, just the same. I think we ought to see her and give her a chance to explain.'

'No, Mike,' Sylvie said, obstinately. 'It's not only that day in London, when she wouldn't see us to say good-bye. It's other things. The day she came to Elmdale and only stopped a minute at your aunt's.'

'Well, she was doing a flying visit. I don't suppose she has much time to spare,' Mike defended.

'Your aunt didn't seem to think so,' Sylvie pointed out. 'She was telling me she thought Penny was a bit peculiar. Stiff, if you know what I mean. Making the visit because she thought she ought to. Your aunt seemed to think she was jolly well relieved when she heard we were out, so she wouldn't be able to see us.'

'Oh, Aunt Flora's hurt about it too, and she's imagining that things are worse than they are,' Mike said, miserably. 'Why don't you write to her? Tell her you can't understand it at all. Ask her if she can see you. Then, if it's only lack of time that's making things difficult, she'll say so.'

Sylvie was silent, thinking that one over. Just then, a young couple paused near them, to look at the sea. The girl, in sun glasses, was leaning on the rail, wistfully watching the children below.

'Well, we've still got the fun-fair to do, Robina,' the young man said. 'Or maybe you'd like to go out in a boat?'

Sylvie wouldn't have taken much notice, but the girl answered, and at the sound of her voice, Sylvie swung round.

Penny hadn't noticed Sylvie and Mike. She turned to walk off with Joe Addy, saying as she went: 'Oh, Joe, I don't think I want the fun-fair. Let's go on the pier.'

'That's funny!' Sylvie said turning back to Mike. 'That was Penny's voice.'

Mike frowned.

'It was like her voice,' he allowed slowly, 'but of course, it couldn't have been her. You heard the chap call that girl 'Robina'. Besides, you know very well that Penny's on the stage at this moment, in the Pier Pavilion at Willowbeach.'

'She might not be on! She might have cancelled her show or something,' Sylvie reasoned.

'But she wouldn't be walking about Redsands with a chap we don't know, who's called Joe,' Mike said with equal reason.

'She might!' Sylvie retorted.

'Well, she wouldn't be being called Robina, now would she?'

Sylvie had to agree with that.

'No, I suppose you're right,' she allowed. 'Oh, I'm being silly. I'm trying to think that — well, it just hasn't seemed like our Penny to go on like the way she has, and — no, it must be Penny who's treating us so offhandedly, and not someone else in her place. How could it be?'

Sylvie dismissed the fantastic idea that had crept into her mind, to explain Penny's attitude. But Mike looked thoughtful. Now he began to experience a little nagging doubt. They had all, his aunt, Sylvie and himself, felt that the Press photographs which had appeared in the newspapers hadn't been like the Penny they knew. Had they been so wrong, after all?

★ ★ ★

Paul had a couple of hours to spare that afternoon, and he decided to go to Redsands to see where the Corn Flakes people were at that moment. He thought of enquiring at the hotel where Penny had stayed but, when he got to the railway station, he saw by the bills on the hoardings, that they were at Willowbeach.

Paul, however, had no idea that Audrey Bayfield had expected him to spend his two free hours with her. She was furious, therefore, when she found he had gone off without a word to anyone.

'Did he say where he was going?' she asked the manager of the music department.

'No, Miss Bayfield, but he'll be back at four o'clock. He is playing tea-time music in the restaurant.'

Audrey nodded and walked away.

'He's with that Penny Maxwell,' she told herself, her anger mounting. 'If I can put a spoke in her wheel I'll do it, even if I have to wait for ages. I'll show her, the little upstart!'

Audrey was wrong in thinking that Paul was with Penny. He had learned that the Corn Flakes company were now at Willowbeach, which wasn't an easy place to get to without a car, in the time he had to spare. The bus journey, involving two cross-country changes, would have taken too long.

Moodily he strolled along the promenade at Redsands, angry to think that his short spell of freedom would be wasted.

He sat down, feeling wretchedly alone, and lit a cigarette.

Suddenly he sat bolt upright. Almost within touching distance Penny walked past him, talking earnestly to a young man he had never seen before. So absorbed was Penny in what she was saying that she had no idea that Paul was so near.

'No, no more, Joe!' she protested. 'We've only been here twenty-four hours and I'm worn out. Let's just walk quietly, or sit down.'

'But I thought you'd like a gay time, Robbie! What's got into you, just wanting to walk and sit about?' Joe asked in amazement.

Penny flushed and bit her lip. Of course, that was just what Robina would want to do — go on everything, and never have a minute that was not packed with entertainment.

'I like looking at the sea,' Penny protested.

Joe looked thoughtfully at her.

'All right, since you want to,' he agreed. 'I've been wanting a quiet talk with you for some time.'

Penny was alarmed. Of course he would want to sit and talk to her, she thought, in dismay. What an idiot she had been to suggest such an idea! It was the last thing she wanted him to have the opportunity to do. He would be sure to ask her to marry him.

But Joe didn't do anything of the sort.

Instead he said hesitantly:

'I've been meaning to ask you about this for some time, but we never seem to get a minute to ourselves. You see, I've been seeing a lot in the newspapers about a girl who won a competition, with her photo in the Curly Corn Flakes contest. Called herself by another name, but she looks like you and, well — was it you, Robina?'

Penny was aghast. It was the last thing she had expected Joe Addy to say.

Joe stared into her astonished face.

'Maybe I shouldn't be asking you point-blank like this,' he said slowly. 'See, I'm the sort of chap who only has one girl. It's been you Robbie, ever since I first saw you.'

'Please, Joe,' Penny protested faintly.

'You know very well it's true,' he persisted. 'You never gave me much encouragement, I'll grant you that. But you can't blame a chap for hoping. And then there was the competition result, and your picture in all the papers.'

He waited and, as Penny didn't speak, he got out a cigarette and lit it.

'Mum said it might not be you,' he went on, not looking at her. 'But I'd swear there isn't another girl like you in all the world. Maybe I'm daft, but that's the way I look at it.'

Penny held her breath, wondering what would come next.

'See, Robbie,' Joe went on, still looking away, 'I was so sure that you'd tell me at once of your good fortune. It's the sort of thing you were always dreaming up. Cut up, mum was, when you never said anything.'

Penny made a movement with her hand as if to stop him from going on, but he didn't notice.

'I knew you had something big on, by way of a job,' he continued, looking down at the smoking tip of his cigarette. 'You went out first thing in the morning, and never came back till late, and you seemed all different in yourself. Then when you said you'd come away with me for this week, Mum said something was up. She guessed you'd had a row with the Corn Flakes people. Is it all busted up, Robbie — your new job, I mean?'

'Oh, Joe, please, I can't tell you now,' Penny gasped.

'Well, there must be something funny about it. I know for a fact you're supposed to be at the Pavilion at Willowbeach. It's on all the hoardings.'

Penny remained silent and, after a

moment, Joe went on. 'All right, you don't want me to know about the competition but, now I do, can't you tell me a bit about it? Maybe I could help you if you've come unstuck with them.'

'Joe, you're a dear,' Penny said, warmly, 'but you don't understand, and there are very good reasons why I can't explain now. One day you'll hear all about it but, for the moment, let's leave it, shall we? Don't let's spoil your holiday. And believe me, I would have told you all about it, from the very first, if I had been able to.'

Joe seemed half persuaded by her earnestness, and then he shook his head in perplexity.

'See what I mean, Robbie! Even this isn't like you. I expected you either to tell me or laugh at me for only just finding out about it. Or else have a row with me for mentioning it, and tell me to mind my own business! I never expected you to be like this about it!'

Penny got up in desperation.

'Joe, I think perhaps I *would* like to do something else after all. I think I'd like some tea somewhere.'

Joe looked rather sullen, but he got up quietly enough and took her arm, and found a table for two in the open-air restaurant and got her some tea. But Penny knew that the matter wouldn't rest there.

11

Robina was annoyed. She had got ready for her appearance at the Flower Show that afternoon, and found that the new dress she had been provided with, was almost severely simple, a tailored blue silk two-piece suit with a small matching straw hat. Not her style at all, but it would have suited Penny perfectly.

That set her thinking of Penny and of Penny's good fortune in being the winner of the competition. By the time Walter Wiley called for her, to take her to the Flower Show in the company's car, she was feeling thoroughly discontented, and her mood showed clearly in her face.

'Hallo, what's the matter with you, Robbie?' he asked, pulling her to her feet and kissing her.

Usually Robina liked his attentions

but today she pushed him away.

'Don't!' she said sharply, 'you'll spoil my make-up.'

Walter Wiley frowned and sat down thoughtfully in a chair by her dressing table, watching her apply more face powder.

'What's wrong, Robina?' he asked quietly. 'Come on, out with it! It's no use thinking you can go to the Flower Show in that mood. You've got to be smiling and gracious.'

'Oh, yes, smiling and gracious, holding the fort for dear Penny Maxwell, so that she can collect the rest of the good things when I'm gone on my way and forgotten. Fine!'

'So that's it. Aren't you getting enough out of this?'

'You know I'm not! I think it's a rotten shame that I can't have all that modelling work and the other things she'll be picking up. After all, I've been doing the hard work, the work she wasn't capable of.'

'Who says she wasn't capable of it?'

Walter Wiley returned, narrowing his eyes. 'I've no doubt that if you hadn't turned up Penny Maxwell would have done her best. Oh, don't sneer at the idea! She would have done very well in her quiet, sweet way. She's sincere, at least, and she'd have done all that was required of her, with a bit of help.'

'Then why did you ask for me back?' Robina shouted.

He leaned forward.

'By bad luck, you started the kind of thing that only you could continue. Having begun that sort of approach, making the audience sing and all that, it would have given the game away if Penny herself had gone on afterwards and just quietly played the piano. But you know all that as well as I do.'

'Yes, I know all that. And I know very well that it wouldn't suit your book if I walked out now, in the middle of the programme. Now, what do you think of that?'

He got up, weary of these scenes with Robina.

'All right, so it's going to be awkward for us. You'll walk out and leave us flat if we don't let you have what you want. What is it you're wanting now?'

Robina's expression changed. She saw that he was going to listen to her, rather than have the programme spoiled by her walking out and leaving him flat.

'I want a car.'

'But, bless me, you're taken everywhere by car now.'

'I mean my own car, to keep, after all this is over and you all say goodbye to me. And I want to choose my own clothes, not those simple things that would suit only Penny Maxwell. The evening gowns are all right — they're my style — but these day clothes aren't. And I want to keep all these new clothes afterwards. I don't want to go back to the things I'll be able to afford.'

'Anything else?' he asked in a dangerously quiet tone.

'Yes. I want a fur coat.' She watched him carefully. Had she gone too far? Or would he laugh and tell her she had some hopes?

'Walter, I don't want to be a trial to you,' she said, beginning a slow, winning smile that only she was capable of, 'but if you got me just these things, then you'd never have another worry about me walking out on you. I'd promise.'

She slid her arms up round his neck but, instead of kissing her, he pushed her off, rather impatiently.

Picking up the little handbag that exactly matched the blue shoes Robina wore, he opened the door of the room and held it for her to go out. They were already late.

'You'd promise, would you?' he said slowly. '*If* I got the things you wanted, you'd have to make that promise — and, what's more, I'd want it in writing.'

They drove in silence to the Flower Show and there was a stiffness about his manner which made Robina feel that she had won that particular battle, but after this she must be careful.

After her duties were over she managed to get away from Walter Wiley, and wandered through the flower tents, basking in the smiles and interested looks of people who recognised her.

'Hallo, Robbie,' someone said, in a deserted corner of one of the marquees.

Robina spun round, expecting to find one of Flash Farwell's boys waiting to take her back. But it was Joe Addy.

Joe had suddenly made up his mind to run over to Willowbeach, to see why Robina wasn't with the Corn Flakes show, but could find time to spend a few days of his holiday with him. He hadn't expected to find another girl exactly like her — having left behind him the girl he thought was Robina.

Furiously Robina faced him.

'Joe Addy, what are you doing here? You're spying on me! Can't you leave me alone — ' She broke off, appalled, as she saw the change slowly creep over his face.

'*You're* Robina all right,' he said,

convinced now that he was right. 'That's the way you always talk to me. Then who's that *other* one, the one who's all polite and considers my feelings?'

Robina hastily tried to cover up her mistake.

'I'm Penny Maxwell — ' she began, but she saw that it was no use. Joe was slowly shaking his head.

'You can't put me off like that, Robina. I recognised you a minute ago. I thought I'd pop over from Redsands, just to see if it was you. I don't know what all this is about, but — '

'Now listen, Joe,' Robina said quickly, looking round. 'People are beginning to stare. I can't talk to you here. Where are you staying? I'll look you up. I'll tell you the whole thing — but not *now*.'

'I'm staying at 5, Gurney Terrace. That's in Redsands. But if you ever *do* look me up I shall be surprised.'

'You'll see. Now go, Joe, there's a dear. Look, they want me. 'Bye for now!' And Robina slipped away to join some people who were obviously looking for her. On her lips was that bright, insincere smile, which Joe Addy knew so well.

He went back thoughtfully to Redsands. He wondered what the other girl would say — the girl who was pretending to be Robina, and who was obviously Penny Maxwell. He had decided, when she had said she was too tired to go out that afternoon, to go secretly on his voyage of discovery. Now he wasn't so sure that that was the right thing. Perhaps he would tell her what had happened. Face her with it, so that if Robina didn't come and explain, he'd get the truth from the other girl.

★   ★   ★

While Joe was in Willowbeach talking to Robina, Penny lay in the little hammock in the back garden, where an old apple tree made pleasant shade over a small patch of grass.

She let her eyelids droop and was almost asleep when their landlady came out and said she was wanted on the telephone.

Wondering who it could be, Penny went into the house and picked up the receiver. It was Joe's mother on the line, calling from London.

'Robina? I'm so glad I caught you in, duck. I thought it might be important. A man called Wiley wanted you on the line. When I said you were at Redsands for a holiday, he said would I let you know he wanted you again. He said you'd understand.'

'Oh, yes, thank you, Mrs. Addy,' Penny said.

'Is that to do with your new job, duck?' Mrs. Addy wanted to know.

'Yes,' Penny said nervously.

'Well, it's a shame, coming in the middle of your holiday.'

'Oh, I don't mind,' Penny assured her. 'Joe's run me off my feet. He's gone out now, while I'm resting.'

She rang off then, before Mrs. Addy

could think of anything else to say but, as she replaced the receiver, she wondered what Walter Wiley could possibly want now.

Penny telephoned him before Joe got back. Walter Wiley had just returned to his hotel from the Flower Show and was delighted to hear from her.

'It's something only you can do, Penny, I'm afraid, or I wouldn't have roped you in again. Do you know Wesley's Store in Sherwood Bay? Do you? Good! Well, they want to tie up with us over a stunt they're running. A song that a chap called Paul Hambledon, on their staff, has written the music for. The public have to find the words, but they think your appearance will pep it up. Will you do it?'

Penny's pulse began to race, because this would mean seeing Paul again.

'What would I have to do?' she asked.

'Seems they want you to sit in the window, for the crowds to look at, and get inspiration for the words to the song. You just have to smile. It's easy.'

'Is that all?' Penny asked doubtfully.

'Well, not quite all — all you need to worry about, anyway. People will know about you, winning our competition, and I'll walk you about the Store for the public to speak to. And there'll be a bit of a party afterwards. You can't say that's difficult, now can you?' Walter Wiley asked persuasively.

'All right,' Penny found herself saying. 'I'll do it.' She was shocked to find that she wanted a real excuse to see Paul again, after having written him that letter.

Walter Wiley gave her the time and other instructions, and rang off, just as Joe Addy came in.

It wasn't till then that Penny wondered what she would say to Joe to explain her appearance at Wesley's, but she didn't have to.

The minute she saw the expression on his face she knew that something had happened.

'What's the matter, Joe?' she couldn't resist asking.

'I thought I'd go and see why it was you weren't parading for the Corn Flakes people at the Flower Show, seeing you won their competition,' he said stonily.

'But you didn't tell me you were going to do that!' she exclaimed.

'No. I wanted to see for myself. Well, I have. You're not Robina.'

Penny spread helpless hands. So the secret was out. It was useless to deny it.

'I've just seen Robina,' he said flatly. 'She got rid of me with the promise to explain everything. She won't though. I know her. And I don't suppose it's any use expecting you to have the decency to tell me what's been going on.'

'That isn't fair,' Penny said quickly. 'I told you — I *would* tell you, if I were allowed to. It isn't for me to say. I'll find out if I can tell you everything, now you've discovered there are two of us.'

'Don't bother,' Joe Addy cut in. 'Seems I've been pretty much of a fool all round. Taken for a ride by the pair of you. Even if you didn't consider you could tell me about it, the least you could have done was not to have pretended to be Robina.'

He reddened as he said it, and Penny was embarrassed, too. He was thinking of the times he had nearly proposed to her believing she was Robina.

'I'm sorry, Joe. I did try to stop you saying things that weren't meant for me.'

'Forget it,' he said roughly, going past her.

'Where are you going?' Penny asked.

'To pack.'

'But why? Your holiday isn't nearly finished.'

'Do you think I can carry on like this any longer?'

'Well, Joe, you stay and I'll leave here. It isn't right that you should lose your holiday as you've worked so hard for it,' Penny said.

'What does it matter to me now?' he retorted. 'After being made a fool of by you two girls I never want to see Redsands again.'

'But what about Robina? You love her, you said you did!' Penny urged, genuinely distressed.

'Did I? I've made myself a doormat to her long enough. It takes something like this to bring a chap like me to his senses. Well, now I'm through!'

He went upstairs to his room and Penny could hear him banging about. There was nothing she could do about it. It was sheer bad luck that he had found out.

Penny decided that she, too, would have to go back to London, after her appearance at Wesley's Store. There was no point in losing any more music lessons, if she couldn't help Joe and Robina any longer. She would have to leave Mrs. Addy's house, too. Obviously she couldn't stay there, and she'd have to find out what Robina wanted to do about her room.

Robina didn't seem to mind when Penny telephoned her to explain what had happened.

'He'll come round,' Robina said

airily. 'He always does. Actually, I'm glad you managed to make him go home — it's saved me awkward explanations. Don't worry about the room. I'll see to that when this business is over.'

Penny heaved a sigh of relief. Now she could undertake her appearance at the Store with no complications about Joe Addy.

There was a lovely new outfit for this special occasion — a cool green and white striped silk, with a little green hat and white accessories. It was simple and in excellent taste, and Walter Wiley thought how fresh and unspoiled she looked and how different from Robina. Penny wasn't at all nervous, for Walter made it easy for her and everything went with a swing.

Audrey Bayfield was there, too, and at the reception afterwards, it seemed that she would never leave Paul Hambledon's side. But eventually he managed to have a word with Penny.

'About this date of ours,' he began,

'you should have told me you were otherwise engaged. I would have understood.'

'I don't understand,' Penny stammered. 'It was perfectly true what I said in my letter.'

Paul frowned. 'What letter, Penny?'

'The one I wrote to you, explaining why I wasn't going to meet you the next day. I had no idea you were going to be engaged to Miss Bayfield soon. As for me, I'm not otherwise engaged. I don't know what gave you that idea.'

'Look,' Paul said urgently, 'there's a lot I don't understand here. How about that date, after all? If you're free, I think we ought to sort a lot of things out, don't you?'

He had just arranged to go swimming with Penny early next morning when Audrey came back. She darted a quick, suspicious look at both of them.

Penny went back to Redsands walking on air. She couldn't imagine what had happened about the letter she had written to Paul, but it was all right now.

He wanted to see her. He was to cycle into Redsands and go swimming with her at seven next morning, and have breakfast with her at a little inn he knew outside Redsands, before he went to work at Wesley's Store.

★   ★   ★

Audrey Bayfield was worried. She had been almost forced to climb down and contact the Corn Flakes people about Penny's appearance, in connection with the song competition. She hoped against hope that they wouldn't allow Penny to do it, and she was filled with anger when she heard from them that they considered it a very good idea for some two-way publicity.

When her anger had subsided, she was afraid. If Paul and Penny got together, Penny would tell him about the letter she had written to him, and she would certainly tell him about the things Audrey had said to her the night of the dance.

The thing to do was to keep them apart, Audrey decided. It ought to have been easy but, at the last moment, she had been called away and, in her new capacity as the owner of the Store, she wasn't so free to stay by Paul's side all the time.

When she came back she caught something that Penny was saying in her clear little voice. Something to do with 'tomorrow morning early'.

Audrey couldn't imagine what they had arranged, and she dare not ask Paul outright.

Finally, the only thing she could think of was to tie Paul up for the time between waking and going to his job at the Store.

'I'd like to go riding, Paul,' she said. 'You promised we should, before breakfast one morning. I can only manage tomorrow. All right for you?'

'I can't, Audrey,' he protested at once. 'I'm sorry but tomorrow isn't possible.'

'Why not, Paul? What could you be

doing at that time in the morning that can't wait?'

'Well, I've got to see someone,' he said quickly.

She was silent and then she said coldly:

'I believe you're just making excuses because you don't want to go riding with me. Isn't that it?'

'No, of course it isn't,' he protested.

'All right, then, it's settled,' she told him. 'We go riding tomorrow. I'll call for you at six o'clock in my car, and you'll be back in good time to have breakfast with me.'

He was suddenly angry. He knew why she was doing this but nothing would persuade him to reveal the fact that Penny was the 'someone' he had arranged to see.

'I'll ride with you, my dear, but I insist on making my own breakfast arrangements,' he said firmly, and Audrey knew she wouldn't be able to shake that decision.

Next morning she thought out

another plan. She galloped ahead and, taking a longer road round, successfully delayed him so that there was hardly time for him to get any breakfast before going to the Store.

Penny, meantime, had been waiting for Paul at a quiet end of the beach at Redsands. She had managed to borrow a bike, to cycle with him to the inn for breakfast after their bathe. The morning was already deliciously warm. Penny changed, and waited, sure that he wouldn't be late.

At last she began to grow uneasy, when it didn't look as if he would come after all. He'd probably forgotten about the date he had seemed so eager to make the previous day.

Tears of disappointment stinging her eyes, she decided not to waste the opportunity for a bathe. The sea looked so inviting.

She ran down to the edge and plunged in, swimming with leisurely strokes out to the end of the pier. She didn't hear Paul call to her. He had just arrived as she ran down to the water's edge.

Quickly he threw off his riding clothes, under which he wore black swimming trunks, and plunged in after her. He was a powerful swimmer, and had almost caught up with her, when she turned off towards the pierhead.

Paul shouted. There were dangerous currents round the piles of the old pier. Scarlet notices were up, forbidding swimming round the pierhead at all; but perhaps Penny didn't know that.

He swam faster, but he couldn't get near in time as she made a slight jerking movement and flung up one hand. Even as he put an extra spurt into his stroke he saw Penny's head disappear.

12

Audrey Bayfield bit her lips in annoyance. She hadn't been able to hold Paul, despite her trick. He had followed her as she took that longer way through the woods, and had said nothing when she pulled her horse in, saying they would rest for a while.

He knew it was a trick to keep him from that appointment about which he wouldn't talk. When they finally reached Sherwood Bay again, he had merely said: 'I'm pretty late, Audrey. I won't have time for breakfast, after all. Goodbye. See you at the Store.'

He had gone from the stables on his bicycle, leaving her to go home alone in her car. She could do nothing. She had deliberately tried to keep him from an appointment, but that was as far as even Audrey Bayfield felt she could safely go, with Paul.

She sat for some time in her car, fuming. Where was he going? To Redsands, instinct told her, to see Penny Maxwell. Why, at this early hour of the morning?

Curiosity overcame her. Slowly she drove out on to the high road, in the direction of Redsands. The white ribbon of road stretched ahead of her, and she could see a lone cyclist.

Driving slowly, keeping him in view, she followed Paul Hambledon right through the busy part of the town and on, watching with amazement when he got off his bicycle at last, at the very end of the promenade, where the beach finished just above the old pier.

Audrey pulled in at the kerb and watched him run down the steps, shouting to a solitary swimmer who was about to plunge into the water. From her car, Audrey saw Paul fling off his clothes and go in after the girl, whom she instinctively knew was Penny.

So that was it. That was the reason

Paul had left her — to go swimming with Penny Maxwell!

A tide of mad jealousy swept over Audrey, leaving her breathless. How could she break up their little party and spoil their pleasure?

A gentle chug-chugging became gradually louder. A small motor craft was nosing into a jetty near at hand. Audrey shielded her eyes and recognised the craft and the owner. She pressed the horn button and waved.

Rick Sanderson was an old friend of her father's. He watched Audrey as she hurried down the beach.

'Anything wrong?' he called, as she ran down the jetty.

'Will you take me out there, Rick?' she asked, pointing to the old pier. 'Don't ask me why — I'll tell you in a minute.'

Into her mind came the half-formed plan of pretending that she thought those two were in difficulties. If she could find an excuse to break in on their private swim, neither of them would find much pleasure in continuing.

'By jove, so that's what you had in mind — they *are* in difficulties!' Rick Sanderson ejaculated suddenly.

He altered course and pepped up his speed. Audrey saw Penny's arm go up and her head disappear, as her companion spoke.

Her heart sank. This wasn't what she had in mind at all. What would Paul say when he found out that she was so near to him, after he thought she had gone home to breakfast, Audrey wondered?

Paul, however, was in no condition to wonder about such things. By the time they reached him he, too, was almost exhausted with holding Penny up and fighting the dangerous currents himself.

'Hold on, we're coming,' Rick Sanderson shouted.

Audrey wasn't much help. It was a tricky business getting Paul and Penny out of the water. Rick did most of the rescue work, leaving Audrey to hold the wheel.

'You'll find blankets in the locker,' Rick called over his shoulder, as he took over from Audrey. 'And some brandy.'

'Thanks,' Paul said. 'Thanks for everything.'

'Don't thank me — it was Audrey who saw you both, and got me to bring the boat out.'

Paul swung round, and recognised the other person in the launch. So far, he had been merely dimly aware that there was someone else in the craft.

Audrey smiled.

'I don't know what you'd do without me, Paul,' she said, in a teasing voice, and went on smiling at him, despite her seething, inward anger.

Penny didn't come to until they had tied the boat up, and Rick was bending over her applying artificial respiration. She looked up in bewilderment at the kindly face of the older man, and then at Paul who, with a blanket round him from the motor launch, was ready with some brandy.

'Paul!' she whispered.

Paul looked angry and frustrated. This was intended to be a quiet time together, straightening out a lot of things that lay between them, still unexplained.

Now, owing to Audrey, it was all spoilt. If she hadn't delayed him, he could have stopped Penny from swimming out to that dangerous patch of water, and this wouldn't have happened. And, to crown it all, Audrey had to be quite unaccountably near at the time, to join in the rescue.

Penny was staring up into his face.

'You saved my life,' she said.

'No, I didn't,' Paul said shortly. 'Miss Bayfield did that!'

'Miss Bayfield?' Penny repeated, bewildered.

Audrey sauntered over from where she had been standing, a little apart, and Penny saw her for the first time. Her face fell.

'You should have waited for me, before going into the water,' Paul told Penny shortly, too furious to venture to say anything more.

Penny bit her lip. It was unfair. He had left it so long that she thought he wasn't coming and, when he did come, he wasn't alone, as he had arranged but, with Audrey Bayfield and her friend.

Penny closed her eyes and told herself she was a fool to have come at all. Didn't all this make it quite clear that Paul Hambledon only regarded her as an ordinary acquaintance and that his real interest centred round Audrey Bayfield?

★   ★   ★

Penny packed up her things as soon as she was able. She felt she would be glad to get back to London again, although she wasn't looking forward to the evening she would have to play the piano at the Red Shoe.

She was preparing to go, when her landlady said there was someone in the parlour asking to see her.

A girl in an extremely smart dress, wearing sun glasses, was standing staring out of the window.

She turned at Penny's entrance and took off the glasses.

'Robina?' Penny gasped. 'What are you doing here?'

'Joe Addy gave me this address,' Robina spoke quickly. 'I've got to talk to you.'

'What about? I'm catching a train to London. I haven't got long.'

'I won't keep you long,' Robina assured her. 'I'm in a bit of a fix. It's Flash Farwell.'

'What about him?' Penny asked, sharply.

'Well, he thinks I'm the one who's been playing the piano at The Red Shoe. He came down to see me last night. He wants me to do an extra job. It's a good thing I was able to catch you before you went back to London — I mean that would have ruined everything, if you hadn't been briefed. He would have guessed there were two of us.'

Penny shrugged.

'I don't see why he shouldn't know, Robina. It's only for the sake of the publicity campaign that it's got to be kept secret, and he isn't likely to make it public.'

'I don't want him to know!' Robina flared. 'You don't understand.'

'You're right. I don't understand,' Penny returned, heatedly. 'And I think it's about time you explained a few things.'

'What are you getting mad about?' Robina asked in a surprised voice. 'You haven't got anything to be worried about!'

'Oh, haven't I?' Penny retorted. 'As if it wasn't enough, with Joe Addy — now you want me to take on something else. I don't mind helping people but, after all, we are strangers.'

'Oh, no, we're not!' Robina said calmly. 'That's the whole point. I wouldn't dream of asking a stranger to do things like this for me.'

'What do you mean?' Penny asked

blankly. 'Of course we're strangers.'

'My dear girl, don't you think it's a little odd that we should be so very much alike and I've found out that we even came from the same orphanage. Doesn't that convey anything to you?'

Penny merely looked bewildered.

Robina went on, with a fine casualness that didn't give away how nervous she felt about trying to put over this story on Penny, 'Doesn't it suggest to you that we might be sisters? Adopted by two different people who each wanted one baby? It isn't unknown for children to be separated when adoption is taking place.'

'Sister!' Penny gasped. 'Oh, no! I don't believe it!'

'Do you hate the idea so much?' Robina smiled. 'It wants a bit of getting used to, I'll admit. But there it is!'

Penny drew a deep breath.

'Look, I'll have to let this train go. I can't be rushed into anything like this. I must hear more about it. When did you find out? How did you find out? Why

210

didn't you tell me before?'

'No, you mustn't lose your train,' Robina said quickly, looking at her watch to hide the alarm in her face. If Penny let her train go, in order to question Robina about this story, she would discover that Robina had no proof, and she would guess that Robina had made it up for her own purposes.

'I could get a later . . . ' Penny began but Robina cut her short.

'No, I'll tell you what I'll do. I've got my new car outside. I'll run you to the station, and tell you more on the way.'

'I'll be glad of a lift,' Penny admitted, 'but I must hear first what it is you want me to do.'

Penny went and got her case, and said good-bye to her landlady, while Robina went out to her car.

When Penny went out of the little house, she wasn't prepared to see the luxurious car which Robina was waiting to drive.

'Is that *yours*?' she asked Robina.

Robina couldn't help smiling with satisfaction.

'All my own,' she assured Penny. 'I got it for helping the Curly Corn Flakes people.'

Penny got in beside Robina, without another word. Somehow Robina was frightening. The things she said, the things she did, were so outrageous.

It was a short run to the station, but Robina was brief.

'Flash Farwell runs a business, besides the club,' she explained. 'All he wants me, or rather you, to do is to go out one evening with one of his clients, and to deliver an envelope for him. That's all!'

'Why can't someone else do it?' Penny objected. 'One of his clerks, for instance?'

'Because the client's seen the girl playing the piano in The Red Shoe and wanted her to go and no one else,' Robina explained.

'I don't like the sound of it,' Penny said.

Robina pulled up in the station yard.

'You don't really think I'd ask you to do something that was going to be, well, unpleasant, do you?'

'I don't know,' Penny said slowly. 'Come to that, why don't you do the job yourself?'

'How can I? You know how tied up I am at this end, doing a job you yourself can't do,' Robina pointed out.

Penny had to admit the justice of that.

They faced each other, Penny still unwilling to agree.

Robina held her breath, watching Penny's doubtful face, and waiting for her to say that she simply didn't believe that they were sisters, and that she wouldn't do the job.

Then a train whistle broke the silence and Penny seemed to make up her mind.

'I'll do it, but this is the last time. You understand that, don't you, Robina? That doesn't mean that I am convinced that we are sisters, either. I must go into that later. And even if we are sisters, I refuse to do anything else for you after this.'

13

Walter Wiley wasn't happy. If the luck went his way, the success of this tour should stand well in his favour for the directorship which had been hinted. But Robina was a trial.

Standing staring gloomily out of his hotel window, he saw Robina's car come along the promenade. Robina was not new to driving, but this car had gone to her head. She drove it too fast. People stared and people were talking. He had heard them. People thought that that car was a personal present from him to the winner of the Corn Flakes competition. Walter Wiley didn't like that.

Robina came up in the lift. He could hear her heels tap-tapping down the corridor. He went to his door and opened it as she passed.

He noticed that she was looking none too pleased.

'You've cut it fine again, for this evening's show,' he warned her.

She whirled round on him.

'You leave me alone! I said I'd walk out on you if — '

'You promised, however, that you wouldn't, once you'd got the car and the fur coat and one or two other expensive knick-knacks,' he reminded her smoothly.

She flushed, and shrugged her shoulders.

'If you must know, I've just driven Penny Maxwell to the station. She's going back to London.'

That interested him and took his mind off the scolding he had been giving her, as she had fully intended.

'I wish you two girls wouldn't be seen about together,' he said quickly. 'The directors wouldn't like it.'

'Oh, it's all right,' Robina said impatiently. 'She's gone back now, and I don't supose she'll be down here again.'

'Who says she won't be?' he countered.

He went back into his room, his shoulders hunched crossly. Robina followed him in.

'What are *you* worrying about?' she asked softly. 'I'm doing the job well, aren't I? A little bird whispered that this publicity stunt has gone so well that you're going to get suitably rewarded. Well, then, why always be picking on me?'

He swung round.

'Who told you that? And for heavens' sake don't follow me into my room. If you don't mind being talked about, I *do*!'

'Why should you?' she asked him, swiftly. 'You're a bachelor, aren't you. You can do as you like, can't you?'

'It happens that I don't *like* you coming into my room,' he said, propelling her out by the shoulders.

'Why don't you? You come into my room!' she retorted.

'You,' he said, prodding her gently with one finger, 'happen to be known as Penny Maxwell, the girl in the public eye. Yours is a suite, with everyone drifting in and out, and there's usually a maid knocking around, if you need a chaperone. It's altogether different.'

Robina drew in a deep breath, to let out an angry rejoinder, when he went on :

'And while we're on the subject, people seem to think that *I* gave you those costly presents. You aren't thinking that, by any chance, are you? I thought I made it quite clear that the company made those gifts to you, to keep you sweet and stop you walking out on them.'

'Oh, no, Walter, I know you gave them to me,' Robina said, softly, smiling provocatively up at him. 'You're only saying the company did it, because you're too modest to admit making a girl such nice presents.'

'I didn't give them to you, Robina, and you know it!'

'All right, I believe you,' she said, backing away down the corridor, 'but thousands wouldn't!'

One of those people who didn't believe it was Audrey Bayfield.

Under the impression that Robina was Penny Maxwell, she watched her with Walter Wiley in the cocktail bar of the most expensive hotel in Redsands that evening, after the Corn Flakes show.

Robina was wearing yet another lovely gown, a black velvet. It's clever cut made Audrey writhe with envy. It was lovelier than anything she had herself.

Audrey was puzzled. It seemed to her that when Penny Maxwell wore these wonderful clothes, she became a different person; provocative, intensely attractive to men — all men in the room, and not only Walter Wiley.

Audrey was with other friends. Paul had gone back to his room to work on his music. Audrey was well aware that the conversation all around her was of Penny Maxwell, seated there at the bar with Walter Wiley who, rumour had it, was going to be a big noise in the Corn

Flakes company in the near future.

As if it wasn't bad enough to have all this adulation, Penny Maxwell had to fill Paul's thoughts, so that he no longer cared how Audrey spent her spare time!

Making an excuse, she got up and went to the cloakroom and repaired her make-up while she thought quickly. As an old school-friend of Audrey's had once said that she knew *Mrs.* Walter Wiley, Audrey wondered how she could turn that fact to her own purposes. At last, a secret smile spread over her face.

She got up and flicked through the telephone book. Finally she dialled a London number and was soon put through.

After she had chatted for a few minutes, Audrey casually introduced the subject that had caused her to make that telephone call.

'Mary, darling, didn't you once say you knew a *Mrs.* Walter Wiley? You did? Well, that would be the mother of the Curly Corn Flakes publicity manager, I suppose?'

'No, don't be silly, Audrey — it's his wife. Why?'

'Oh! Oh, no, you must be mistaken,' Audrey said, in a concerned voice. 'The man I'm thinking of is here, in this hotel, flirting outrageously with that girl who won their competition. You know the one I mean. Oh, no, you must be mistaken, Mary, because I've just remembered — rumour has it that he's bought her that new car she's seen about in, to say nothing of a fur coat I'd give my eyes for and — '

'No-o!' the friend breathed from the other end of the line. 'Do you think . . . '

She trailed off delicately.

'No, I'm sure he must be a bachelor,' Audrey said quickly. 'You've got mixed up, darling. Your Mrs. Wiley must just be a relation, not his wife. Forget what I said. It's all quite, quite confidential, mind! Not a word to anyone. Promise!'

'I promise, cross my heart!' Mary, at the other end, purred. Audrey knew, from schoolday memories, however,

221

that when she promised like that, it was a matter of minutes before she called up everyone she knew, to pass the information on, under a plea of its being confidential, and not to be mentioned.

Audrey went back to the ballroom feeling a lot better. Penny Maxwell wouldn't find life so easy, she thought smugly, when her old friend Mary got busy.

But Penny Maxwell had troubles of her own. She had to go back to the Addy house to pick up some of her things. She chose a time when Joe would be at work, but she couldn't hope to evade his mother.

'Well, miss, what have you been doing to upset my Joe, *this* time?' Mrs. Addy demanded, her jolly face no longer friendly.

'Hasn't he told you, Mrs. Addy?' Penny asked, carefully.

'No, not a word can I get out of him,' Mrs. Addy said.

'Then I had better not say anything.

Don't ask me. Believe me, it's for the best, this way.'

At that moment the telephone in the hall downstairs began to ring. Mrs. Addy went down to answer it.

'It's for you,' she called up to Penny.

'That you, Robbie?' Flash Farwell's well-remembered voice came over the line, as Penny picked up the receiver.

Her heart began to beat unevenly. She answered him as casually as she could, and waited, but she was totally unprepared for his next words.

'What's the idea, Robbie? Are you trying to double-cross me, as well as those Corn Flakes people?'

'What do you mean?' Penny whispered, her heart in her mouth.

'What I say,' Flash Farwell returned, his voice harsh. 'First you're here in London, playing about with me, pretending to be a shy girl up from the country. Then you're down on the coast parading about in that publicity stunt.'

Penny caught her breath.

'Look,' she said. 'I can't talk here. I

shall be seeing you tomorrow night.'

'Oh, no, you're not fobbing me off like that,' he said sharply. 'All right, you can't talk where you are. Well, I'm in the callbox at the end of your road. Just walk down there to me, and no tricks. It's time we had a little talk.'

Penny replaced the receiver and picked up the small case of things she had brought down with her.

She saw Flash Farwell just coming out of the call box. He had been watching down the road.

'What's that for?' he asked at once, pointing to the week-end case she carried.

'I'm changing my digs,' Penny said.

'What for? What's the idea?' he asked sharply.

'I don't want to stay there any longer.'

'Why? Fallen out with them?'

'Look,' Penny said desperately. 'Surely I can go and live somewhere else without having to explain to any one?'

He laughed shortly.

'Not likely! What, and run out on me again? Don't be silly — as if I didn't know you, Robbie!'

'I'll give you my new address when I get it,' she urged, 'but I just can't stay there any longer. The landlady's son is being tiresome. It's very embarrassing.'

'What's wrong with you?' he asked, in genuine surprise. 'I've never known you to run away when it came to handling a boy-friend! Well, you'd better come and live at my place, then.'

Penny's head shot up, startled, and she said quickly, 'I couldn't do that!'

'Why not? You've done it in the past — why not now?'

Despair filled Penny's thoughts. Just what had Robina been in the habit of doing, before she met Penny?

Flash Farwell dug his hands deep in his pockets and his expression was almost kindly.

'You haven't had a fall, knocked your head or something, have you, Robbie?' he asked on a gentler note.

225

'Of course not!' Penny exclaimed. 'Why?'

'Because I don't understand what's wrong with you if you haven't. It strikes me you're acting as if you've lost your memory or something — you don't seem to recall anything that's been happening between us. If you're acting, then I'll hand it to you, you're doing fine! But be careful,' he said, in an altered tone. 'Don't play with me too much. You ought to know by now that it just doesn't pay.'

'What do you want me to do, then?' Penny asked, dully.

He was right, of course. For the time being, at least, she must go easy, where he was concerned, but for a reason he didn't know about. If Penny didn't take care, he would do just what she and Robina didn't want him to do — he would discover there were two of them, and that she herself wasn't the girl he wanted!

'Stay where you are for a start,' Flash Farwell answered decisively. 'I don't see why you need to clear out and I'm suspicious of your wanting to. For another thing, I'm interested to know what your game is with those Corn Flakes people.'

'I don't see why I shouldn't make money on the side, when I'm not working for you!' Penny said with spirit.

That seemed to please him. He grinned.

'That's better. I can understand you when you give up acting the shy little country girl. Now, what I wanted to see you about was this. The job I wanted you to do, remember?'

As Penny nodded, he went on: 'For reasons which I don't have to tell *you*, we've got to go quietly on that. We'll put off that little party for the time being. Just turn up at The Red Shoe as usual. Oh, and this week it'll be a bracelet I want you to drop. Get me?'

Again Penny nodded, and waited. But he said no more. With a satisfied jerk of the head he turned and walked off.

Forced by Flash Farwell to stay on at the Addy house, Penny made up her mind to make the best of it.

She found it was uncomfortable taking meals with Joe's mother as usual but, as Joe himself kept away, it wasn't unbearably embarrassing.

A few days later, Robina forwarded an envelope addressed to Penny, post-marked Elmdale.

It was an invitation card. Mike and Sylvia were to be engaged, and were to have a party in two day's time at Wesley's Store in Sherwood Bay.

Just a formal invitation, Penny thought, choking back the lump which rose in her throat.

But Sylvie had once been her best friend. After a great deal of thought, Penny decided she would go, and wrote at once accepting the invitation.

As Walter Wiley had once asked her to do, she telephoned him, to let him know that she would be in the district for the party, and the time she would arrive.

'Oh, glad you let me know, lass,' Walter Wiley said. 'We haven't got a show on that evening, so I'll take Robina out of it, so the two of you won't be seen. I'll take her up to London for dinner and a show.'

'How's the show going?' Penny asked him.

'Fine. Couldn't be a greater success,' he said cheerfully.

When she arrived at Wesley's in a taxi from the station, on the evening of the party, her spirits lifted a little.

Sylvie, in a white dress, came forward to greet Penny and tried not to seem uncomfortable.

'Penny! I didn't think you'd be able to come! How are you?' Sylvie said.

'Sylvie! I'm so happy for you and Mike,' Penny said warmly. 'Of *course* I was able to come — I wouldn't have missed your engagement party for anything! Hallo, Mike, how are you?'

Sylvie looked faintly surprised as Penny spoke.

'What's the matter?' Penny asked.

Sylvie looked distressed.

'Of course it's Penny. There isn't any doubt about it,' Mike said and, turning to Penny, he greeted her with the same awkwardness that Sylvie had shown.

'We were having a bet,' he said to Penny after a slight hesitation. 'Sylvie didn't think it was you.'

A wave of alarm swept over Penny. She was well aware that they thought she hadn't been behaving like her usual self. It was a surprise to her, however, to find that they were now wondering if it had been Penny at all.

'I'm leading a strange life,' she said, rather breathlessly, trying to make an explanation without giving too much away. 'If I don't seem like my old self, don't take too much notice. Personally, I'll be glad when all this is over.'

'Aren't you enjoying all those wonderful clothes and the good time?' Sylvie asked at once.

Mike broke in before Penny could answer that.

'I didn't know you could drive, Penny.'

Taken unawares, Penny said quickly: 'Oh, I can't.' Then, realising the slip she had made, she amended it: 'I mean I can't drive well.'

Before Mike could say anything more about the car, people began to come up and speak to her. In no time, Penny realised that she was the celebrity of the evening. Everyone recognised her and Penny thought in dismay that she stood in danger of stealing the limelight from Mike and Sylvie.

Looking round for a chance to escape, her face changed. She blanched as she saw Paul Hambledon walk quickly across the carpeted floor. He was in evening dress and looked more handsome than ever. He looked neither to right nor to left as he hurried by and Penny didn't know whether he had seen her or not.

'What's Paul Hambledon doing here?' she asked Sylvie.

Sylvie darted a quick look at Mike as she answered.

231

'He's playing the piano in the orchestra for the dancing. The regular pianist is still away. Didn't you know that, Penny?'

'No!' Penny exclaimed. 'How could I know that?'

Sylvie looked queerly at her.

'Well, perhaps I shouldn't mention it, but I saw him leaning over the side of your car the other day, in Redsands, talking to you. There's no mistaking that mauve car.'

Penny caught her breath. Robina! What could Paul have had to say to her?

'I didn't know he was playing the piano for your party, Sylvie,' Penny said quietly.

The party was an ordeal. Penny danced a few times with Mike, but he seemed stiff and unnatural.

Miss Bailey sat out and said a few words to Penny but, all the time, Penny felt a barrier between her old friends and herself.

'We didn't think you'd come, to tell you the truth,' Miss Bailey admitted.

'We often see you, gadding about in that new car of yours that the Publicity Manager gave you.'

She pursed her lips as she said it, and Penny flushed.

'The company made the gift,' she gently corrected Miss Bailey. 'They seem very pleased. It seems to have been a greater success than they anticipated.'

'It's a very costly gift, to show their appreciation,' Miss Bailey remarked shrewdly but inoffensively.

'I've no idea what made them do it,' Penny said, with truth, 'but it occurs to me that it might be as much for advertisement as it was a gift. Everything they do seems to be for advertising purposes.'

'Oh, well,' Miss Bailey said. 'I suppose I'm an interfering old woman. Why should I worry if there's been a lot of talk about you? I suppose you know what you're doing, and it's none of my business.'

Before Penny could reply, Paul

Hambledon came over and asked her to dance.

Reluctantly she left Miss Bailey. Much as she wanted to talk to Mike's aunt, it was a relief to get away at that particularly tricky part of the conversation.

Paul didn't help matters, with the first thing he said.

'I must be mad sticking my neck out like this.'

'What on earth does that mean?' Penny gasped.

He shrugged.

'The last time I saw you, you seemed to think that everything I said was rather amusing, particularly when I least meant to be amusing.'

Penny closed her eyes. Robina again!

'When was this?' she asked wearily.

'You've already forgotten the time I spoke to you when you were driving that hideous car your pal Wiley gave you?' he said bitterly.

'Look, I've just been telling my old friends from Elmdale that Walter Wiley didn't make me a gift of that car. Why does everyone believe such nonsense? The company provided that, and I agree with you — it *is* hideous.'

'You seemed to be pretty pleased with it, and with yourself, too,' Paul said, still in that unfriendly voice.

'Then if you feel like that, why did you bother to ask me to dance?'

'Because I felt I had to make you believe that it was the truth about why I couldn't get there in time on the day you were nearly drowned. I went so far as to get one of the other chaps in the orchestra to take over the piano just for this number because I was afraid I wouldn't get another chance of speaking to you tonight. You must admit you're getting pretty slick at evading me, when I see you in the street.'

Penny caught her breath. If this was true, then he didn't sound as if he was trifling with her.

'I didn't know you were delayed,' Penny said earnestly, looking up at him. 'I thought you weren't coming at all and that you'd forgotten all about me. Then when you came with Miss Bayfield and her friend — '

'I didn't come with them,' he said impatiently. 'I came on my own, after I got away from her. I'd stupidly promised to go riding one morning with her and she held me to that particular morning. What choice have I? She's my boss. Anyway, you didn't seem to care about the reason, one way or the other, the day you were driving that ghastly car, and I stopped you to explain.'

The whole thing was hopeless. Without his realising that there were two of them nothing could be done to convince him that Penny wasn't just being off-handed. She would have to let him into the secret and chance angering Walter Wiley.

'If I told you that it isn't me you see in that mauve car . . . ' she began, but Paul Hambledon broke in angrily.

'Now I've heard everything! You can't expect me to believe such a tall story!'

'But it's true,' Penny insisted. 'I can't even drive.'

He stared at her for a moment, unconsciously slowing up. The dance finished. Couples all around them stood clapping for an encore, but Paul and Penny stood staring at each other.

At last Paul said, still in that angry voice:

'Oh, why keep fobbing me off with these fantastic stories? Why don't you be honest for once and admit that you blow hot and cold, according to your mood? I could understand that. I suppose it's only natural for all this excitement and gaiety to go to your head but, for goodness' sake admit it, and don't start pretending that some-one else is messing things up for you!'

14

When the party was over Sylvie said to her, 'Where will you be staying tonight, Penny? In Sherwood Bay?'

Penny nearly blurted out that she had decided to go back to London, late as it was, but just stopped herself in time.

Before she could answer, one of the staff came up and said that she was wanted on the telephone.

It was Walter Wiley.

'I wondered if I'd catch you, lass, before the party broke up. Can you stay down here tonight? I'll be wanting you tomorrow.'

Penny knew that she couldn't very well refuse. After all, she was supposed to undertake anything Walter Wiley wanted her to do on behalf of Curly Corn Flakes.

'Yes, I'll stay, but where's Robina?' Penny asked.

'That's the trouble. I don't know,' Walter said, unhappily. 'The things she does! But this time she's gone a bit too far. I took her up to London for dinner and a show, and we hadn't been in the restaurant five minutes before she got up and went out, and I haven't seen her since.'

'But she'll come back!' Penny said quickly. 'Did she see anyone she knew?' she added, wondering if Robina had caught sight of any of her friends in Flash Farwell's circle and had escaped before they could reach her.

'She was in a funny mood. She's been threatening to walk out on us and I daren't take any risks. That's why I want you to stay, in case she doesn't show up for tomorrow.'

'All right, then I will,' Penny replied.

'Good, now go to the hotel where a suite is reserved for Robina. I'll call you in the morning.'

Robina didn't come back the next day. Walter Wiley telephoned to Penny to tell her so, and to make the day's arrangements.

'It's the presentation of the prize for the Song Competition,' he told her rather awkwardly.

'Then you'd want me, anyway, wouldn't you?' she asked in a puzzled voice.

'Well, now look, lass, don't be hurt or anything, but to be blunt, we'd decided to have Robina do this job.'

'Why? I mean, I did the other appearance at Wesley's.'

'I know,' he agreed, 'but that was easy. This really calls for something — well, up Robina's street, shall we say? But now she isn't here in time. I'm afraid we'll have to do the best we can, you and me. Will you try?'

'Of course,' Penny said willingly.

'That's the girl,' Walter approved.

He had no idea what an ordeal that afternoon show was to Penny. Audrey Bayfield was well in the foreground, monopolising Paul Hambledon, who studiously avoided Penny's eyes and looked acutely miserable. It was his music, and the competition was as much his show as anyone else's, and he had composed the music for Penny. But there was no happiness in it for him, the way things had turned out.

A young man had won the competition with his lyric. He came up to the platform where Penny stood, in a dream of a dress, and his good-natured face creased up into a sudden warm smile as he reached her.

Instead of the words he had rehearsed he blurted out:

'Gosh, now I see you close to, you're really *beautiful*!'

Paul sat at the piano, flinching. He had seen a lot of Robina's stage technique, and he waited automatically for her scintillating smile to be turned on, the charm and quick patter, which won people at the time. Instead, Penny smiled her beautiful smile and said warmly: 'How very kind of you to say that.'

'I could write any number of lyrics

about a girl like you,' the young man went on.

Walter Wiley thought it was high time to step in. He introduced him smoothly as Kevin Brady and Penny presented the prize.

'Will you sing my lyric, Miss Maxwell?' Kevin Brady said impetuously.

Walter Wiley looked dismayed.

To his delight, Penny said quickly: 'With pleasure, if Mr. Hambledon will be so kind as to play for me.'

'What are you doing?' Walter Wiley whispered frantically to Penny.

She merely smiled at him and went over to the piano. She had been too shy to handle the audience on that first occasion she had appeared in Robina's place and so it had been taken for granted that she couldn't sing.

Penny, however, could read music at sight. It was essential, too, to make this effort. It was the only thing, she thought swiftly, to convince Paul that she had been speaking the truth when she had tried to tell him that there was another girl who looked exactly like her.

The minute she began to sing, his head shot up and she felt his surprised glance on her. Her singing was completely different from Robina's. Her voice had a richness and sweetness of its own.

Walter Wiley listened with incredulous delight realising that he had underestimated Penny Maxwell.

Kevin Brady, who hadn't seen Robina on the stage, was enchanted; but Paul couldn't wait to get off the stage and ask Penny a thousand questions.

As he watched her, he realised that he must have been blind not to see for himself that this — and not the girl who angered and wounded him so much — was Penny.

Walter Wiley hustled Penny away afterwards, to congratulate her himself, so Paul didn't get a chance to talk to her.

On the way out to the company's car

Walter Wiley was stopped by two other executives, and he had to let Penny go on alone.

But no sooner had she got to her room than the desk rang up to say that someone wanted to see her urgently, someone who said that Miss Maxwell knew her very well.

Penny sighed.

'All right, ask her to come up,' she said, thinking it might be one of her friends.

Penny didn't recognise the smart woman who stood at the door.

'Perhaps you were expecting my husband, Miss Maxwell,' the woman said unpleasantly.

Penny bit her lip. She didn't know what to say.

'I don't — ' she began, but the woman broke in scornfully.

'Don't you? I'm Mrs. Walter Wiley,' she said.

'Mrs. Wiley?' Penny thought quickly but could not recall ever hearing whether Mr. Wiley was married or not.

'I don't understand. Has something happened to him?'

Mrs. Wiley frowned. This was not the reaction that she had expected at all.

'Not that I know of,' she said coolly. 'I think we'd better have a little talk, don't you?'

As she spoke, her glance went swiftly over Penny, from head to toe.

Penny flushed.

'Well, I was going to rest until Mr. Wiley wanted me,' she said, 'but if you really want to talk we'd better go downstairs to the lounge.'

'Why not here? I understand my husband will be coming up when he arrives.'

Penny was dismayed. That must be Robina's way of going on.

'I think there's a little misunderstanding to be cleared up,' Penny said tiredly. 'You'd better come in, after all.'

She ignored the mocking smile that lit the other woman's face and stood aside for her. Mrs. Walter Wiley looked all round, with a cynical expression in her eyes.

'My husband is paying for all this!'

'What nonsense!' Penny exclaimed angrily. 'The Corn Flakes company has engaged this suite and they're paying for the clothes and everything; in fact — it's part of the prize.'

'Don't tell me you're going to say that the new car and the fur coat go with the prize, too,' Mrs. Wiley sneered.

'Indeed, I do, but those were extras for a rather special arrangement that was made.'

Even as she said it, Penny saw that Mrs. Wiley deliberately misunderstood.

'Oh, yes, I think I should like to hear more about that special arrangement.'

'I can't tell you until Mr. Wiley comes,' Penny said. 'It isn't for me to say, but I'm sure he'll explain everything.'

Mrs. Wiley's eyebrows arched.

'I doubt it,' she said. 'Now, after all that nonsense, let us get down to facts. I didn't come to see my husband. I came to see you.'

She sat down, and lit up a cigarette in a long holder. Through a haze of blue smoke she stared insolently at Penny.

'My husband has an unusual job. He get's around. He's met girls like you before and I haven't taken any notice. But this time I've decided that I'm not going to put up with it any longer.'

'Put up with what?' Penny asked.

'Oh, really — don't pretend to be a little innocent. I've heard all about you. You were on the stage before you won this competition. I can't think what the company was about, to present the prize to a professional. It doesn't strike me as being fair. But, apart from that, you're just the type to — '

'Look, let's get this straight,' Penny broke in. 'I was not on the stage. I was in a baker's shop. Anyone will tell you that if you go to Elmdale. I don't think Mr. Wiley would mind my disclosing this much in the circumstances but, the fact is, the girl who was on the stage was merely my stand-in, when I was ill.'

Mrs. Wiley looked surprised and then derision crept into her face.

'Really, it's outrageous! Why don't you admit you've been carrying on a flirtation with my husband?'

'Because it isn't true!' Penny flared. 'Why do you listen to these wicked rumours? Why don't you ask your husband for the truth?'

'Because I know very well I wouldn't get it!' she retorted. 'But I see no reason why he should spend all his money on a chit of a — '

'For the last time,' Penny interrupted angrily, 'he hasn't been spending his own money on either of us!' She stood with her back to the door, bright spots of colour in her cheeks. 'And, although you may find it difficult to believe that there is another girl exactly like me, who has been taking my place, never-the-less it's true. The company didn't want the public to know, naturally. But it isn't so difficult to believe, surely, that two sisters can be so much alike?'

Mrs. Wiley half rose in her chair at that. But it wasn't with surprise at what Penny had said. She had half risen to meet the people who stood at the open door, astonishment all over their faces. They were Walter Wiley and Robina.

Penny swung round to see what Mrs. Wiley was staring at. The last person she expected to see with Walter Wiley was Robina.

Walter Wiley was the first to recover. He closed the door behind Robina, and came slowly into the room, looking at his wife.

'What's the idea, Vera?' he asked, in a stony voice. 'Started following me around again?'

'I'm getting rather tired of hearing rumours about my husband's way of carrying on his job,' Mrs. Wiley said coldly. 'I thought it was time I came to see what the girl was like, but it seems there are two of them!'

Robina's eyes were wide, and angry.

'Did she say she was your wife? Did I hear correctly?' she asked Walter Wiley.

As he nodded briefly, Robina went on furiously, 'Well, of all the low-down tricks! Why couldn't you say from the start that you were married?'

'Now just a minute,' Walter Wiley broke in. 'What was it you were saying, Penny, when I came into the room? Is that true, that you two girls are sisters?'

Penny said steadily, 'Robina found out that we both came from the same orphanage and, it seems, we were adopted by different people.'

'Never mind about whether they're related or not,' Mrs. Wiley broke in impatiently. 'There are one or two things I want to know about, far more than that. Just how much have you been spending on that girl, Walter?'

'For heaven's sake, Vera, not now!' Walter Wiley interrupted. 'I've got other worries to sort out.'

'Well, you're not sorting them out in my suite,' Robina told him curtly. 'I suggest you two go downstairs to the lounge or somewhere. I want to talk to Penny.'

'I don't think there's any point in saying anything else, Robina,' Penny said quietly. 'I've done the job you should have done this afternoon, and I've found out something else you did to mess things up for me. I think the less I see of you the better I shall like it.'

She went out of the room, but Robina hastily followed her.

'What d'you think of that?' she said to Penny, disgustedly. 'Married all the time and hoodwinking me into thinking he was a bachelor with plenty of money! It makes me furious! Wait a minute, I'll walk down with you.'

'Well, since you insist on coming with me,' Penny said, 'you'd better tell me what you said to Paul Hambledon the other day to make him feel he doesn't want to see me any more.'

The two girls faced each other in the wide, deserted corridor of the hotel.

'Oh, he waved to me to stop, and started telling me a sad story about seeing me drowning, and couldn't get there in time to save me. I don't know what it was all about, but it sounded funny, and made me laugh. He was livid!' She looked closely at Penny. 'I say, you've not fallen for him, have you? I shouldn't waste my time if I were you. He hasn't got a bean.'

'I prefer to please myself about the friends I make,' Penny replied evenly.

Robina shrugged.

'Why don't you tell him we're sisters? You told Mrs. Wiley so.'

'Paul didn't believe me when I said there were two of us. And while we're on the subject, what happened to you?'

Robina grinned.

'It so happened that I caught sight of someone I knew in the restaurant, and speed was necessary.'

'Who? Flash Farwell, you mean?'

'No,' Robina said impatiently. 'A producer who once promised me a good part. I thought I'd remind him, but I didn't catch him up till he got out to his car.'

'You mean to say you left Mr. Wiley without any explanation?' Penny asked, genuinely shocked.

'It was my future career, wasn't it? I couldn't stop to explain to him. Anyway it didn't come to anything.'

'Well, I still don't see why you didn't get back here till just now.'

'He drove me out to his house for drinks and then it was too late to catch Walter, so I went back to Mrs. Addy's,' Robina said. 'They'd all gone to bed but the key was under the mat. I slept till mid-day and cleared out while Mrs. Addy was down at the fish and chip shop but I couldn't get here in time for the show.'

'Well, what about Mr. Wiley and his wife?' Penny asked. 'She was out to make trouble.'

'Oh, don't worry about her,' Robina said scornfully. 'She'll let him talk her round. That type always does! Anyway, there's nothing in it for me, even if Walter Wiley does get the directorship they've promised him. I'm out for bigger things and I advise you to take the opportunity of looking for a rich

man, too, and let Paul Hambledon go!
He'll never amount to much!'

15

Paul had been thinking the same thing up till that moment. And then something surprising happened that altered everything. He had been sitting at the piano in the Store, after everyone had gone and the Song Competition was all over, when Kevin Brady, the winner, strolled over to him.

'Are you too busy to see me?' he asked, with that engaging grin of his.

Paul roused himself with an effort.

'No, carry on,' he invited Kevin Brady.

'Well, about this song of ours, we're not just going to leave it at that, are we?' he asked Paul. 'I mean, one popular number, one competition. I don't know about you but I could go on writing lyrics like that until the cows come home. Have you got any more stuff like that?'

Paul stared.

'I never thought about it. I suppose I could go on writing tunes, too.'

'Right! What do you say to us teaming up, then?'

'I don't quite get you,' Paul said slowly. 'So far as I know there isn't much future in song writing.'

'Oh, I know that. I know all about song-plugging. That isn't what I mean at all. What I had in mind was a show. A musical show. We can think up a story — that's not difficult — but it's the song hits in the show that count. The song hits, and the girl. We've got the girl. She's a winner herself, but she's got the Corn Flakes publicity behind her, too. Don't forget that.'

Paul sat back, staggered.

'It sounds all right,' he admitted at last. 'But I don't know anything at all about show business. Do you?'

'I was born in it,' Kevin Brady said, happily. 'I know the ropes but, of course, one can't do much alone. I think, as a team, you and I could do something. Care to try?'

Paul got up, thoughtfully.

'Yes, I'd be glad to,' he said, 'but we can't just barge ahead without consulting the young lady herself.'

'Well, why not do it at once? What time do you finish here?' Kevin Brady asked him.

'I'm through now,' Paul said slowly, 'but I think I'd rather see her alone, if you don't mind. Give me a note of where you're staying and I'll get in touch with you,' he told the disappointed Kevin.

Paul hurried over to the hotel beset with the fear that it would be the other girl he would have the bad luck to see, and not Penny at all.

But luck was with Paul. He ran into Penny coming out of the hotel, alone. She had just said good-bye to Robina, with a feeling of foreboding. Robina was in a dangerous mood.

Paul was the last person Penny expected to see. They stared at each other for a second. Paul was the first to speak.

'It *is* you, Penny, isn't it? Not that other one?'

Penny had a forgiving nature. It wasn't in her to hold it against him, that when she had tried to tell him about Robina, he hadn't believed her. Something had happened to convince him since then, and for her, that was enough.

Her lovely smile spread over her face as she looked up at him, and his heart beat faster. No one but Penny could smile like that!

'Here, come on!' he said, grabbing her hand. 'There are loads of things I want to say to you.'

'But I was just on my way to the station,' she said, breathlessly, and he noticed that she was carrying a small case. 'I'm going back to London.'

'To London?' he echoed blankly. 'Oh, yes, of course. That's how you both work it. One here to carry on and — '

'I see you *do* believe me now,' Penny nodded.

'We must talk. Get a later train,' he

said firmly, hailing a taxi.

Penny stared as Paul, gay as he had never believed he could be, opened the cab door for her and said jubilantly to the driver: 'The Ship Tea-Rooms.'

It wasn't far to the old part of the town, and a quaint little street off the harbour. Their table in the bow window with bottle glass panes, commanded a view of the masts of the fishing boats at anchor.

'This is nice,' she murmured, with a sigh. 'I like it.'

'So do I,' he agreed, and they were still staring at each other, oblivious of everything around them, when the proprietress brought them tea and hot buttered scones. Her kindly smile brought them both back to earth.

'What did you want to see me about?' Penny asked.

'First, have you forgiven me for being such a bear at our last meeting?'

'Of course,' she said impulsively. 'But it *has* been so difficult. You're the first to know the secret. My old friends in Elmdale still don't know what it's all about. They keep running into Robina — '

'The other girl,' he nodded. 'How did you manage to find your own double?'

'She's my sister, she tells me,' Penny said simply. She explained what Robina had told her about being adopted from the same Orphanage by two different families. 'Then, of course, we lost touch,' Penny went on. 'Robina saw my photograph in the newspapers when I first won the competition and contacted me.'

'So it's your sister I've been constantly seeing,' Paul said, trying to sort it all out. 'That explains a lot of things.'

'It was me on the beach when I nearly drowned,' Penny reminded him, 'and me at Sylvie's party.'

She talked on, quietly, straightening the whole thing out for him, and yet unaccountably unable to bring herself to mention the business of Flash Farwell, out of loyalty to Robina and her past associations.

'Now I've found you, I mustn't lose you,' Paul said, gripping her hand. 'Oh, but I nearly forgot what I wanted to see you about. It's really tremendous news! Kevin Brady, the chap who won the competition this afternoon, wants me to team up with him, writing songs for a musical show of our own!'

'Oh, Paul, I'm so glad for you!' Penny exclaimed sincerely.

'Only for me?' Paul's eyebrows went up. 'Don't you ever think of yourself and where you come into it, Penny?'

'*Do* I come into it?' she asked, with a catch in her voice.

'Of course! We want you to be our leading lady.'

Penny's smile slowly vanished. Was this why Paul had said he mustn't lose her again. Not because he cared for her but because she was apparently essential to him for his show?

She slowly shook her head.

'If that's what you want, then it isn't me but Robina who will fill the bill.'

Paul looked staggered.

'Oh, Penny, don't be a little chump,' he said, with a touch of impatience. 'Don't you understand? Brady has never seen Robina on the stage. It's *you* he's heard sing, and it's *you* he wants.'

She glanced away, out of the window and, as she did so, she saw Audrey Bayfield getting out of her car. The commissionaire at Wesley's had heard Paul saying to Kevin Brady that he was going to Penny's hotel, and the commissionaire at the hotel had heard the instructions Paul had given to the cab driver. It wasn't difficult for Audrey to run Paul to earth.

But Penny wasn't to know that. It struck her that Paul must have arranged for Audrey to follow him.

She got to her feet.

'I'll think it over and let you know,' Penny said, gathering together her gloves and bag. 'I'll be getting along. Your friend, Miss Bayfield, is coming in.'

Paul got to his feet but was too late to stop Penny from hurrying out.

'Penny, wait a minute,' he called, but Audrey Bayfield appeared in the doorway, smiling, and successfully blocking his path, so that Penny had time to hail a passing cab and make for the station.

Penny's eyes stung with tears. She hardly knew how she got through the rest of that day. The journey to London, the taking up of the threads of her music lessons again, and the prospect of her next appearance playing the piano at The Red Shoe, gradually had the effect of blotting out the hurt she had sustained after that meeting with Paul Hambledon.

Penny settled down to her neglected work at the music school. The performance at The Red Shoe started quietly enough. Flash Farwell showed no signs of anything out of the ordinary happening, as he fastened the antique bracelet round Penny's slender wrist. The customers were the same sort of people as usual, paying little attention to the girl in the red dress seated up there playing softly to them.

She didn't see Paul Hambledon come in with Audrey Bayfield and her party.

Paul was furious.

'Why did we have to come to this club, Audrey?' he whispered, under cover of the other three people settling with the waiter as to where they should sit.

'My friends chose it, not I,' Audrey said lightly. 'Why? Do you know anything about the place?'

'I know that it has an unsavoury reputation,' Paul said quietly, as they took their places at a table not far from Penny. 'I know people who even go so far as to hint that the proprietor is engaged in drug traffic. I don't like you being seen here. I don't like *any* friends of mine to be seen in a place like this.'

'One of your friends,' Audrey remarked, her eyes skimming the room and alighting on Penny, 'apparently *works* here.'

He followed the direction of Audrey's glance and half-rose to his feet with surprise. He had had no idea where to begin to look for Penny after she had run away from the Ship Tea-Rooms and, yet, here she was — or, was it that other girl?

'Sit down, Paul, people are looking at you,' Audrey urged.

Paul, staring at Penny, decided that it was her and not her sister. Only Penny could be so oblivious to everyone, quietly absorbed in her music. Then she got up, her number ended, and took her bow, nervously fiddling with the ornate bracelet at her wrist.

'I must speak to Penny,' Paul said.

'No, Paul!' Audrey objected, half-rising, angry.

And then there was a sound that caused pandemonium. The lights promptly went out, tables and chairs were knocked over in the sudden blind scuffle to escape from the place.

Paul shouted to the other members of the party.

'Get Audrey out of here! Quick — it's a police raid!'

Penny stood bewildered on the little circular dais, too frightened to move. Then she realised that the bracelet had gone.

She had unfastened the spring clasp, and released it in the way Flash Farwell had shown her. It had fallen, just as the lights had gone out. She was sure that the man who was to have picked it up hadn't been able to do so.

All this flashed into her mind in a matter of seconds. Then a strong hand clasped her wrist and she was tugged along. A familiar voice whispered: 'Come on, Penny. Let's get out this way.'

Paul Hambledon! Gratefully, Penny let him steer her through a small opening, covered by a thick curtain. Up a tiny narrow passage and down some steps, and through what appeared to be a cellar. And then came the blessed, cool night air.

Up the cellar steps Paul tugged her.

Penny had no coat but, almost at once, a taxi cruised along and Paul hailed it.

'I'll get you home, and then I must see what's happened to Audrey,' he said.

Penny gave her address to the driver, chill at her heart. So he had been out with Audrey for the evening! Paul was scribbling down her address in a small book which he put back into his pocket. There was an odd look on his face as he turned to her.

'Why are you living in a place like that, Penny?'

'It was Robina's digs,' Penny said quickly. 'About Miss Bayfield, you haven't left her all alone, have you?'

'Oh, heavens, no!' he said impatiently. 'She's with the rest of the party. She'll be all right. Never mind about her. What about you? What would have happened to you if I hadn't managed to get to where you were standing?'

'I don't know,' Penny said, suddenly aware that she was shaking all over. 'I didn't know the place was likely to be raided. I don't understand.'

'It's got a bad name,' he said flatly. 'What on earth were you thinking of, to take a job in a place like that? Penny, you won a competition. You should have a lot of money from that, and now I find you in poor digs, and working in a night club which is on the list of the police.'

Penny caught her breath.

'There's a simple explanation,' she replied, 'but I don't quite see why you think you should be concerned about me. After all, you're practically engaged to Miss Bayfield.'

'Who told you that?' Paul exclaimed. 'No such thing! She is my employer. What on earth made you think there was anything more to it?'

Penny frowned.

'I seemed to have got the impression from several quarters that there was more to it than that. Miss Bayfield certainly gave me the impression — '

'So that's it!' Paul broke in grimly. 'Well, be that as it may, it just so happens that the only young woman I'm interested in, is about as elusive as can be, and furthermore she has to go and find her own double, to confuse things still more.'

Then, in an altered tone, he said:

'Penny, you're shivering. I left my overcoat behind, too. Here, let me put my arms round you, to keep you warm.'

Her heart beat suffocatingly fast as he took her in his arms, but words would not come.

At that moment the taxi came to a standstill. The driver looked round.

'This is it, guv'nor,' he announced, with a cheerful grin.

Paul nodded, and told the man to wait. He helped Penny out, and waited while she found her key.

'Look, Penny, get your coat and come back with me. You need some food after that shock. Besides, I want to talk to you,' Paul said urgently.

Penny obediently ran quietly up to her room and got a coat. She snuggled into it as she settled back in the cab and listened to Paul giving the name of a restaurant to the driver.

'I hope Robina's coat is all right,' she said. 'I left it in the cloakroom in The Red Shoe.'

'I think we'll forget about the coat and anything else you left behind,' Paul said. 'I hope it didn't have a name tab on it?'

'Because of the police?' Penny took him up, and then clapped a hand to her mouth. 'Oh, but the bracelet! It must have got kicked along the ground in the scuffle. I must go back and find it.'

'What bracelet?' Paul frowned.

Haltingly Penny explained and, as she did so, his brow darkened with anger.

'Do you mean to tell me that you entered into this arrangement willingly?' he asked in horror.

Her heart beating faster, Penny said:

'Why? What's wrong with it? It's just dropping a bracelet — and — '

'Do you really believe that?' Paul asked her urgently. 'Are you sure you

270

got the same bracelet back? Or do you think perhaps this chap has another one just the same, which he gave you, keeping the original?'

'Why should he do that?' Penny asked innocently.

'Penny, what was this bracelet like?'

She described it. 'Heavy, sort of antique, and each piece was on a hinge to the next piece. It's the fashion.'

'Just as I thought. I don't know for sure, mind you, but at a rough guess, each of those pieces, as you call them, was probably a container, and each one was full of the stuff.'

'Stuff? What are you talking about?'

'Drugs. Your Flash Farwell runs the racket but, so far, no one has succeeded in pinning any evidence on him.'

Penny was thinking quickly.

'You mean, then, that I was passing it to that man, and he gave me back a bracelet that looked the same, but was just an ordinary bracelet really?'

'Exactly. What else could be the explanation of that nonsense, Penny?

Ask yourself! Why — why, in heaven's name did you ever start doing it?'

Her eyes were anguished as she raised them to his.

'Flash Farwell thought I was Robina. He was threatening. So, as Robina was doing my job for Curly Corn Flakes, I agreed to play at The Red Shoe for her.'

Paul snorted. 'Robina! The more I hear about that girl the more difficult I find it to believe that she's your sister. We'll have to go into this Penny. I think a visit to the Orphanage, perhaps with our family solicitor, might be of use. Meantime, there's a telephone call I have to make.'

16

When they arrived at the restaurant, Paul telephoned to Audrey's hotel to find out if she had got home all right. As Penny stood quietly by him, she saw his face change.

'D'you mean to say she hasn't arrived yet? But what happened?'

He listened without speaking and then, with a few words of commiseration, he put the telephone down.

'What is it?' Penny asked.

'It's Audrey's father, terribly upset. She's been arrested.'

'But why?'

'They weren't as slippy at getting away as we were,' Paul said. 'Audrey and the rest of our party were picked up with most of the other guests. It would have been all right, just their names and addresses taken, but it seems that Audrey was wearing a bracelet which interested the police.' He looked at Penny. 'A plain clothes man pounced on it. It seems they knew a little of what was going on, but they wanted proof.'

'*Wearing* it!' Penny remarked, almost incredulously. 'She must have picked it up having felt it on the floor with her feet, in the dark — that's if it was the one I had.'

Paul knitted his brows.

'Is that what a girl would do, Penny, if she found a bracelet — fasten it on her wrist?'

'I suppose so, in a muddle like that, until she could hand it to someone. Why didn't she explain all that to the police?'

'She did,' Paul told her. 'It seems that if she'd been holding it, they might have believed her. But *wearing* it!' He frowned. 'Well, there's nothing more we can do to help her.'

'Oh, yes, there *is* something we can do, at least, I can. I must go to the police and tell them what I know about the bracelet!'

'Penny! D'you realise what might happen?' Paul asked sharply. 'I can't let you do this for Audrey.'

'I'd do it for anyone,' Penny said quietly.

* * *

Robina had a visitor next day. It was Paul Hambledon.

'You didn't expect to see me, did you?' he said, as she gaped at him. 'I expect you can guess what I've come for.'

'I don't know what you mean,' she flared at him.

'I want you to come back to London with me,' he told her. 'I daresay you've read about the raid at The Red Shoe last night.'

'What about it?' Robina retorted.

'You knew Penny Maxwell was playing the piano there,' he said, accusingly. 'Don't you care what happened to her?'

'The newspapers say that Flash Farwell has been caught, and the rest of his gang,' Robina said shrilly. 'So that's all right. There's nothing more to worry about.'

'Oh, yes, there is. Miss Bayfield was caught with a certain bracelet loaded with a white powder that I imagine you know all about. She only found it on the floor, after Penny had dropped it, but no one would believe that until Penny offered to go to the police and explain.'

'She did that?' Robina gasped. 'What an idiot! She'll have us all in trouble. It's nothing to do with me! I don't know anything about it!'

'Oh, yes, you do,' Paul insisted. 'You know so much that it was to save your skin that Penny Maxwell took the job on in the first place. She's got Miss Bayfield out of the clutches of the police, and now you're coming to get your sister free.'

'Not me,' Robina said. 'If Penny Maxwell's stupid enough to get into this mess, then she can get herself out of it. And she's not my sister.'

'You told her that you were her sister,' Paul said.

Robina sneered.

'I know I did! It was a good story, and she swallowed it. It answered the purpose. She thought it was her duty to go and take over from Flash Farwell for me. Her sense of duty makes me sick. And there's no need for you to look like that at me — I helped her out where the Corn Flakes competition was concerned.'

'You did very well out of it, too,' Paul remarked. 'A car, a fur coat, to say nothing of a wardrobe that cost the earth. And if you want to go on doing well out of it, you'd better get Walter Wiley to release you from your engagement for today and come with me to London. Don't panic! It's merely to assure the police that there are two of you looking exactly alike. That will just make Penny's story believable.'

Robina stared at him.

'You must think I'm as simple as she

is. What you want me to do is to put my head in the police station, to get hers out, don't you? I know I've got nothing to fear — I've never handled the drug jobs, and I've never touched anything else that was criminal. But who'd believe that, if I admitted that I'd known people who had?'

She started to dab powder on her nose, her back turned to him.

'Robina,' Paul said softly, 'I'm afraid I'm going to have to insist on your coming to London, to do this for your sister.'

Robina whirled round on him.

'She's not my sister, I tell you.'

'She *is* your sister,' Paul said, with conviction.

Robina looked uncertainly at him.

'What d'you mean?'

'I must confess that I found it absolutely incredible to believe that Penny Maxwell could have a sister like you,' Paul said heavily, 'so I got my solicitor to find out more about it. The Orphanage assures him that, strange as it may seem, you and Penny really are sisters.'

'I don't believe it!' she stormed.

'That being the case, I shall have to do pretty much what your pal Flash Farwell did, to make you see reason. I promise you that if you come with me my solicitor will see you through. You'll give the information to get Penny released, and you'll remain free yourself — if it's true you haven't done anything criminal.'

'All right,' Robina said sullenly. 'I'll come.'

★   ★   ★

Penny thought she would never be happier as she stepped out of the train with Paul and Robina.

The police business was behind them, all cleared up. Flash Farwell and his gang had been caught. And there was no more need to keep up that horrible pretence — everyone could now know about herself and Robina.

It was true that Walter Wiley still didn't want them to be seen about together, but Penny was only coming back to Elmdale for the week-end. Then she was returning to London to take up her music lessons in earnest. Audrey Bayfield had gone abroad at once with her parents, after The Red Shoe incident. Robina would go back and finish the publicity appearances. Paul was to work on his musical show with Kevin Brady. And Miss Bailey and the others could now be let into the secret.

Penny glowed with happiness and looked forward to delicious week-ends with Paul and her old friends.

One lovely Saturday they went out to his old home. They stood side by side in the stable yard, staring at the desolation, and a lump came into Penny's throat.

'Why don't the new owners move in, if they're going to? Why leave it empty, to go to ruin?' she asked.

'They found Tyler's Holt would take too much money to convert it to their purposes, after all,' Paul said quietly. 'It's now up for sale again. Up for sale, my home, and I haven't the money to buy it back!'

'But your musical show — if that's a success, you ought to make more than enough to buy it back, Paul!' Penny said warmly.

'*If*,' he said, bitterly. 'It would be nice if we could ever put it on, but first we have to get money to float it.'

'I can help,' Penny said. 'And I would play in it without payment.'

'I can't take things from you, Penny. The money you got from the competition is for your music lessons and I couldn't let you play the lead for nothing. It isn't sense, and I can't have it.'

Tears pricked Penny's eyes. If he really cared at all for her, surely, he wouldn't mind taking her services and her money? They would be given with all the love she had had for him for so long. But no mention of his own feelings for her had ever been made. He seemed to want to be just friends.

'One day there'll be a lot of money to buy back your home,' Penny said. 'Money to float your show. Money coming in all round.'

He looked quickly at her.

'What makes you so sure?'

'I know it. I feel it, way deep inside me,' she said.

'Oh, a presentiment,' he said, brushing it aside as of no importance. 'I'm afraid I'm not given to having presentiments. I'm the practical kind, I suppose. I see no hope of any money and, heaven knows, I've tried. So, those being the facts, I accept them.'

'You make it all sound so gloomy, and it isn't, you know. There are lots of bright, happy things happening. For instance, your home is up for sale again, instead of having been turned into something perfectly frightful that would hurt you every time you looked at it. And you and Kevin are writing the most wonderful songs that will be smash hits one day. And then there's

Mike and Sylvie's wedding.'

'Doing your best to cheer me up, aren't you?' Paul, laughed softly, as he ruffled her hair.

The last Curly Corn Flakes show, far down the coast, finished. Penny settled down to an autumn of hard work on her music, when one day, about two months later, Walter Wiley sent for her at the Curly Corn Flakes London offices.

He greeted her warmly and settled her in a comfortable chair.

'We thought,' he began, 'my directors and I, that it would be nice for us to stage something for you in the nature of a thank-you to our competition winner and all that. A charity show in Sherwood Bay, the proceeds to go to your local hospital. What do you say, lass?'

Penny was thrilled and touched by their kind thought.

'But what about Robina?'

'I thought of her,' Walter Wiley admitted. 'But I expect she's off and away on that stage career she's always talked about, isn't she? She wouldn't want to be bothered, would she?'

'I think she might like to come in on this,' Penny told him, 'if she's free.'

'Well, that's fine,' Walter Wiley said. 'She can do her old act. She was jolly good at it. You can sing your song, the one that young Hambledon and Brady did for the Wesley Song Competition, and you can play the piano. And we'll introduce Robina as your sister who's on the stage. That'll be all right.'

Penny hadn't seen Robina since the police business over the night club but, when she wrote to her about the charity show, Robina accepted at once. She admitted that she hadn't any stage work.

She appeared to be friendly and Penny decided to be content with that. They made their performance a success, both dressed alike. The whole charity show went off very well and both girls got good Press notices.

'It ought to set you both up very nicely,' Walter Wiley said. 'I wonder you two don't do a sister act together.'

'That's a wonderful idea!' Penny exclaimed. 'For Paul's show, I mean.'

Before Robina could say a word, Walter Wiley pricked up his ears. 'What show is this?'

Penny launched into an enthusiastic account of what Paul and Kevin hoped to do. Walter Wiley listened with interest.

When they said good-bye to him he didn't say anything, however, except to wish them both luck.

Penny was to be a bridesmaid at Sylvie's wedding, and Paul, best man. And so, on that lovely Autumn day, with the sun making gold and crimson beams through the windows on to the mellow stone floor of the aisle of the little old grey church, Sylvie in her bridal white was married to Mike Bailey, and Paul Hambledon rose to the occasion as best man, and little Penny Maxwell stood demure in blue velvet, as the chief bridesmaid.

Miss Bailey beamed at her and at the happy pair.

As the bridal procession came down the aisle again, Paul fell into step beside Penny, and there was a new glow in his eyes.

'Penny,' he whispered, 'did *you* speak to Walter Wiley about our show?'

She blushed guiltily and, as the bridal pair met the barrage of confetti and rice outside, she said, 'Well, I did mention it to him. Did you mind?'

'Mind,' Paul almost shouted. 'My dear girl, it was a brainwave — it was a brilliant idea. He's going to float the show for us — he, and his company, that is. They want the publicity but, as far as I'm concerned, they can have it! We're getting the money we needed, *and* the theatre, *and* the blessing of the Curly Corn Flakes Company, *and* — '

The two little bridesmaids, in a panic, hissed at them to move on. Photographs were to be taken outside. Among the Press photographers was Mike's own assistant. They wanted a group, and Penny and Paul were hustled into place.

After the group was taken, and the people began to move, Paul grabbed Penny's arm.

'Penny, will you marry me?'

'Oh, Paul, what a place to choose to ask me!' she stammered, in confusion.

'It's the best place in the world. Outside a church, weddings in the air, everyone bursting with happiness, and — best of all reasons, it happens to be in the first flush of knowing that I'm not going to be hard-up for the rest of my life. I couldn't ask you when I had no money, Penny, my dearest, but now it's different. Penny, will you marry me, my dear?'

Penny's 'yes' was almost lost in the laughter and the hustling away of the bride and groom in their car, but Paul heard it.

★ ★ ★

Later, when Paul and Penny were alone, walking in the deserted ground of Tyler's Holt, Penny said thoughtfully;

'What are we going to do about Robina? Will you have her in the show?'

'It'll all work out,' Paul prophesied, happily. 'She's good at her particular act, as we all know. And, thank goodness, Wiley and his wife have made up their quarrel over her.'

'You mean you're going to let her do her own act in the show?' Penny breathed.

'You wouldn't be happy if I didn't, now would you?' Paul told her, smiling gently at her. 'It'll give her her chance. Then there's you singing the special songs we'll write for you. And you and Robina with your sister act. All good revue stuff; just what we want.'

'What will you call the show, Paul?'

'I think — ROAD TO ROMANCE.'

He smiled contentedly, as he drew her into his arms.

We do hope that you have enjoyed reading this large print book.

Did you know that all of our titles are available for purchase?

We publish a wide range of high quality large print books including:
Romances, Mysteries, Classics
General Fiction
Non Fiction and Westerns

Special interest titles available in large print are:
The Little Oxford Dictionary
Music Book, Song Book
Hymn Book, Service Book

Also available from us courtesy of Oxford University Press:
Young Readers' Dictionary
(large print edition)
Young Readers' Thesaurus
(large print edition)

For further information or a free brochure, please contact us at:
Ulverscroft Large Print Books Ltd.,
The Green, Bradgate Road, Anstey,
Leicester, LE7 7FU, England.
Tel: (00 44) **0116 236 4325**
Fax: (00 44) **0116 234 0205**

Other titles in the
Linford Romance Library:

SECOND CHANCE WITH THE PLAYBOY

Charlotte McFall

At thirty, Annabel Simpson is the youngest doctor to take charge of a ward in the history of Oakwood Hospital. A possible closure threatens her position and spurs her into action. Organizing a charity bike ride from Brighton to Land's End seems like a good idea — until she is paired with her wayward ex, Marcus Chapman. But Marcus has changed, still grieving the loss of his daughter, and is determined to break down the barriers Annabel has erected. Can they find the courage to mend their broken hearts?